'Why did you do that?' Laurel said in distress.

'Because I wanted to. Because I've wanted to for a very long time.'

There was sincerity in his voice, but she was still unsure. 'Really? Or is it because you find it amusing to see if I'm available?'

His eyes looked steadily into hers. 'And are you available?'

'No!'

'So now we know where we stand, don't we?'

THE
GOLDEN GREEK

BY
SALLY WENTWORTH

MILLS & BOON LIMITED
ETON HOUSE   18-24 PARADISE ROAD
RICHMOND   SURREY   TW9 1SR

*First published in Great Britain 1991
by Mills & Boon Limited*

© Sally Wentworth 1991

*Australian copyright 1991
Philippine copyright 1991
This edition 1991*

ISBN 0 263 77368 X

*Set in Times Roman 10½ on 12 pt.
01-9112-51931 C*

Made and printed in Great Britain

CHAPTER ONE

IF THE loose stone hadn't been there none of it would have happened. It became the pivot of her life. Laurel was carefully carrying a large tray of shards down from the dig to the museum, her arms stretched out almost to their full width, so that when she stumbled over the stone she was unable to regain her balance. Her first thought was for the pieces of broken pottery that had been so laboriously unearthed, and she tried desperately to save them as she fell. Luckily the tray was a deep one and Laurel managed to keep it steady, but in doing so she fell heavily and awkwardly, sending a stab of pain shooting through her right wrist.

She cried out, and several nearby tourists rushed to help her, asking if she was hurt in a variety of languages.

'It—it's my arm,' Laurel gasped, then gritted her teeth against another wave of pain.

A burly, middle-aged German helped her to her feet, but she had to lean against him, fighting off black clouds of dizziness. 'Where you go?' he demanded. Unable to speak, she managed to raise her left arm to point down to the museum, and he swung her up into his arms with a grunt of effort. Someone else rescued her precious tray and she was carried in a small procession through the throng of interested tourists who made way for them. At the museum she pointed the way round the back to the workrooms where her fellow students were standing at the long benches, washing and numbering the finds. Seeing them arrive, the Greek in charge of the workrooms came hurrying forward and, getting his priorities right, first took the tray and then found a chair for Laurel. Over her head, everyone began explaining what had happened, but it gave her a few minutes in which to recover a little, so that she was able to lift a pale face and thank her helpers warmly before they went off, their visit to Delphi made even more memorable.

Her wrist wasn't broken, but it was badly sprained. It was strapped up and put in a sling. 'And you are not to use it for two weeks,' the local doctor informed her. He sounded very blasé and bored, as if he handed out the same instructions several times a week. Which he probably did with all the tourists climbing over the site in unsuitable shoes so that they constantly fell and hurt themselves.

'But I'm supposed to be working on the excavation,' Laurel explained in dismay.

'So now you will just have to lie in the sun and rest.' But he gave her a smile, his eyes not unaware of her tall, slim figure and mane of tawny hair.

The idea wasn't unattractive; after all, that was what most tourists came to Greece to do, but all the other students staying in her hostel were working on the dig during the day, so that Laurel was left entirely alone. She tried going to the workrooms with the others, but was forced to ask for help to do even the smallest task and she became a nuisance. And when she just sat and chatted with the other girls she distracted them from their work, so that she was banished, though kindly, back to the hostel. After a couple of days of this she was thoroughly bored, tired of reading and with no more friends and relations she could send letters or postcards to, laboriously written with her left hand. Going through her address book yet again, Laurel came to a page of scrawled signatures and telephone numbers of students she had known during her first year in college but who had left for one reason or another. She stopped at one, 'Niko', followed by a telephone number with the codes that she recognised for Greece and Athens.

Niko? Laurel lifted her face to the sun, trying to remember. Why, of course. He was the Greek student who had been at college for only a year to brush up on his classical Greek before taking an exam. Quite tall and dark, she recalled, and good fun to be with. She hadn't known him terribly well—he was a couple of years older and just one of the crowd she had gone around with in that summer term—but in the general euphoria of an end of year party Niko had signed her book and told her to look him up any time she came to Greece. Well, she was in Greece and very much at a loose end. Without giving it much further thought, Laurel went inside to the phone and awkwardly rang the number.

A man's voice answered in Greek and she said, 'Hello? Niko?'

Switching to English, the man said, 'Who do you want to speak to?'

'Niko.' Laurel consulted her address book and tried to read the signature. 'Niko Alexiakis.'

'I'm afraid he is not here at the moment. If you will give me your name and telephone number perhaps Mr Nikolaos will be able to contact you when he returns.' The voice was smooth, practised, as if he repeated the same thing a dozen times a day.

It put Laurel's back up, but she gave the number of the hostel, her name, and added that she had been a fellow student of Niko's. It didn't change the man's attitude; he merely said goodbye and put the phone down. Disappointed, Laurel went back to her chair in the dry, dusty garden behind the hostel, convinced that her phone call had been a waste of time.

The other students came back from the dig that evening, tired but cheerful, eager to shower and have a meal. They were a mixed bunch from half a dozen countries, but were nearly all classical scholars who had volunteered to spend part of their summer vacation working at Delphi, either at the current excavation or at the museum. At dinner they sat at long tables, hungrily tucking into salad served with Greek feta cheese, and helping themselves from large serving dishes of moussaka. It was far from luxurious, but the food was good and plentiful, which was all they asked for.

Halfway through the meal the Greek who ran the hostel put his head into the dining-room and yelled out that Laurel was wanted on the phone.

'Hello?'

'Laurel? It's Niko.'

'Oh, hi. Do you remember me?'

'Of course. We were at college in England together.'

Laurel laughed, not believing him, as she'd already given him that piece of information, but pleased that he should pretend. 'I'm surprised that you do; it's been over a year since you left college.'

Niko smoothly changed the subject. 'Are you in Greece on holiday?'

'No, I'm working. Well, doing voluntary work, that is. I'm in Delphi for the summer.' She laughed.

'Although I'm not even working now because I've been really stupid and sprained my wrist, so I'm pretty useless to them at the moment.'

'So you thought you'd give me a ring.'

'Well, you did say to look you up if ever I was in Greece,' Laurel pointed out.

'And I'm glad you did. Look, I'm only in Athens; I can't make it tonight, but how about if I drive over and pick you up tomorrow morning so that we can spend the day together?'

'That sounds great. But what about your job; will they give you the time off?'

'That's no problem,' he assured her in what sounded like amusement. 'Tell me where in Delphi to find you.'

Laurel described the position of the hostel and he promised to be over at about eleven. Grinning to herself, Laurel added, 'You won't have any trouble recognising me—I'll be the one with her arm in a sling.'

Niko laughed and said warmly, 'I'm looking forward to tomorrow. *Kalinichta*, Laurel.'

''Bye.' Smiling, Laurel replaced the receiver and found that she, too, was looking forward to tomorrow.

Niko was late, but only a little. Laurel was sitting in the shade of an olive tree outside the hostel and her eyebrows rose when he turned up in a white, open-topped Mercedes. Her memory of him had been correct; he was tall for a Greek and had thick, curly dark hair, his handsome, olive-skinned face deeply tanned, but he looked far more prosperous than she remembered. His clothes were designer casual and there was a gold watch on his wrist, a thick ring on his finger and a heavy medallion of the same metal round his neck. He was wearing sunglasses, so that she couldn't see his expression, but he gave an 'Ah,' of satisfaction as he got out of the car and looked her over as she stood up to meet him.

'Confess,' Laurel teased as he took her hand. 'You'd completely forgotten who I was.'

Niko grinned at her, his head only slightly taller than hers, completely self-assured. 'I wasn't quite sure what you looked like, but I remembered your voice,' he told her. 'It's so unusual, so husky for a girl.'

It was a comment that had been made many times before. Laurel extracted her hand from Niko's and gestured towards the building behind her. 'Would you like a drink? They have cold beer or Coke.'

He gave the hostel a rather disparaging glance. 'No, thanks. Let's go.'

He helped her into the car, solicitous for her comfort, and asked her how she'd hurt her arm. Laurel told him as he started to drive away, and she made him laugh as she described the incident, exaggerating a little to bring out the comic side of it. She paused, enjoying the breeze in her hair, and glanced back. Delphi was behind them now, the white stones of the ruins climbing the grey mountainside, the steep rocks of the Phaedriades, 'the Shining Ones', guarding the holy spring. The spectacle caught at her heart as it always had, right from her visit here as a schoolgirl, a visit that had unshakeably determined Laurel to become a classical Greek scholar. They rounded a bend and Niko, too, looked back. 'Impressive, isn't it?'

'It's more than that,' Laurel returned eagerly. 'There's still a feeling of magic about Delphi. Didn't you feel it?'

'Of course; I'm Greek. We always feel the ethos of a place,' Niko said quickly. But then he shrugged. 'But with so many tourists...'

'I know what you mean—but shouldn't everyone have a chance to see it?'

He shrugged again, ducking the question. 'How long do you have in Greece?'

'I'm booked to work at Delphi for another five weeks and then I planned to have another couple of weeks travelling round the islands.' She glanced at the road ahead. 'Where are we going?'

'To Athens.'

'Really? Is that where you live?'

'Most of the time.' He gave her an amused sideways glance. 'I travel quite a bit.'

'In your job?'

'You could say that.'

'What do you do?'

Again the amused smile. 'I suppose you could say I work for the family firm.'

Refusing to directly ask the question his amusement called for, Laurel said, 'You didn't pursue your classical Greek studies, then?'

For a brief second there was wistfulness in his dark, expressive eyes, but then Niko said, 'No. It wasn't considered—necessary that I should.'

Laurel waited for him to go on, but when he didn't she turned to look out of the window. If Niko chose to be mysterious that was up to him; she certainly didn't know him well enough to probe deeper.

The road from Delphi to Athens wasn't unfamiliar to her, but Laurel had always travelled in a local bus before, usually squashed in among women loaded with enough shopping to last a month, plus all kinds of livestock. So now she looked round with enjoyment, sitting back in the comfortable leather seats of the powerful car as it ate up the miles. Niko was a rather flamboyant driver, taking the bends a little too fast, to impress her, but he handled the car well and she didn't feel at all nervous. She did most of the talking, telling him about the people who'd stayed on at college after he'd left, bringing him up to date on all the gossip.

'Didn't you keep in touch with anyone?' she asked him, recalling a rumour that he'd had a close relationship with one of the other girls in his year.

But Niko shook his head. 'I meant to, but you know how it is.' He gave an expressive wave of his right hand. 'After I came back to Greece I started going around with my old friends again.'

'But didn't you ever see—what was the name of the girl you used to go around with? Was it Carol?'

'You mean Kathy.' His lips tightened. 'No, we lost touch,' he said shortly.

He changed the subject abruptly then, asking Laurel about her work in Delphi, and she got the message that he didn't want to talk about his past.

When they reached Athens he drove straight to a restaurant in one of the best districts, the waiters hurrying forward and greeting him by name. Laurel was surprised rather than impressed. 'You must come here a lot,' she remarked.

Niko gave a careless nod. 'It's one of my favourite eating places.'

His apparent affluence made her a little wary; Laurel didn't go for men who set out to arouse her interest in that way. 'Are they all like this?' she said casually.

'Similar, I suppose. Not that I'd come to dinner here, but it's good enough for lunch.'

Deciding that she didn't much like this side of him, Laurel looked him in the eyes and said, quite loudly, 'Do you remember that time you got drunk at someone's party and you ended up stark naked in the university fountain?'

Niko gave her a startled look, and for a moment she thought he was going to be angry, but then his dark eyes filled with amusement. 'Are you——' he searched for the phrase '—taking me down a few pegs, Laurel?'

'Something like that, yes.'

He laughed aloud. 'I forgot that you were English. Greek girls are more impressionable.'

'And you find it necessary to impress them, do you?'

He looked at her for a moment and again an almost wistful look came into Niko's eyes. 'Sometimes I wish I were back in England again,' he said, his lower lip jutting forward moodily. 'They were good times. I felt free there, with no one watching me all the time to make sure I didn't let the family down. Or almost no one,' he added with a grin of remembrance. 'Stavros was supposed to keep an eye on me, but he told me straight away that I was on my own.'

'Stavros?' Laurel was having trouble managing with one hand, and he leant forward to cut her food up for her.

'A sort of uncle,' he told her, concentrating on his task.

Laurel raised her eyebrows in surprise. 'Are you saying that your family watch you all the time here in Greece?'

'Not that closely, no. But my father has mapped
my life out for me. I am expected to—conform; isn't
that the word? And he likes to know who my friends
are.'

'Is that why you didn't keep in touch with Kathy?'
Laurel asked shrewdly.

He stiffened and for a moment she thought she'd
offended his pride, but then Niko nodded shortly. 'My
father didn't approve.'

She stared at him. 'But what had he got to do with
it? It was your decision, surely?'

Niko gave a rather scornful laugh that twisted his
mouth, but didn't answer until the waiters had taken
their plates away, set the next course on the table and
moved out of earshot. 'You're English; you don't
understand the strength and tradition of the Greek
family. My father is very stern, very strict. I have to
obey him. I'm his only child, you see, so I have to
carry on the family tradition.'

He was right, Laurel didn't really understand, but
she could see that Niko wasn't completely happy despite his apparent wealth. He was only about two years
older than her own age of twenty-one, and she could
guess that he must find it a struggle to 'conform', as
he'd called it. 'Is it worth it?' she asked curiously.

He gave her a peculiar look. 'That's a question that
doesn't even come into it. I am my father's son.'

It would have sounded corny except for the dignity
with which Niko said it. Laurel could suddenly imagine the line of his ancestors going way back in time,
each of them upholding the family tradition, even if
the only real tradition was pride. It matched up with
the ancient Greeks that she studied, their honour and
their patriotism. Thoughtfully, she said, 'Maybe I do

understand, a little.' Then grinned. 'But what if your father disapproves of me?'

'He couldn't help but approve of you,' Niko said gallantly, but then spoiled it by adding, 'And anyway, he's away for a few weeks.'

Laurel burst into laughter and he gave a flashing grin of real humour. 'That wasn't your father who answered the phone when I rang yesterday, then?' she asked.

'No, that was his secretary.' He gave her a contemplative look. 'You've told me about everyone else I knew, but haven't said much about yourself. Do you have a lover back in England?'

With a small gasp, Laurel said stiffly, 'Not right now, no.' And she averted her head angrily.

Niko was immediately contrite. 'Have I offended you? I'm sorry. Perhaps I used the wrong word. I should have said boyfriend. Fiancé.'

But Laurel was sure his English was too good for him to have made a mistake like that. He'd just wanted to test her, to see what her reaction would be. Coolly she said, 'No, not at the moment—even though I'm old enough to choose my own friends.'

That stung, as she'd intended it to. His face tightened for a moment but then Niko gave her one of his most charming smiles, and as he was very handsome it was a most devastating smile. 'You're angry with me. I'm sorry.' Reaching across the table, he took her hand and set out to cajole her back into a good humour. And did it so successfully that Laurel was laughing again when they left the restaurant.

As she'd remembered, he could be good fun when he wanted to be, and an even better companion when he relaxed and forgot about his 'family tradition'.

They had a great time that day, ending up at another restaurant for a marvellous meal.

'Let's go on to a night-club. I want to dance with you,' Niko declared.

'I have to get back to Delphi,' Laurel protested. It was already very late; following the Greek tradition, they hadn't dined until nearly ten.

'What's the point of going back there? I'll only have to drive all the way out there again tomorrow to collect you.'

'Are we going out together tomorrow, then?'

'Most certainly,' Niko told her with an arrogant assurance. 'So why not stay in Athens tonight?' he said persuasively, pulling her to him and kissing her lightly.

But Laurel insisted on his taking her back to Delphi. She had enjoyed the day and didn't want it spoiled by having to fight him off. The trouble with Niko was that he was too darned attractive. She guessed that he had made quite a few conquests among his fellow students while he was in England, and she didn't want him to think that because she was English she was easy. All she wanted was to be friends.

The next day he took her to an exclusive club on the coast north of Piraeus and they went out on his sailing boat; the day after that to the club again, where Niko water-skied while Laurel watched, frustratedly angry that she couldn't join in. 'Never mind,' Niko consoled her. 'I'll teach you as soon as your wrist is better.'

The days passed in an endless round of sybaritic enjoyment. They ate in exclusive restaurants, danced in night-clubs where the drinks cost the earth, went sailing in Niko's beautiful yacht, and sunbathed on beaches so private that they often had the long golden stretches of sand to themselves. And Niko gave her presents: a thin gold bracelet for her wrist, a hibiscus in a tub to brighten her room at the hostel, an evening-gown because she hadn't brought one with her. There were lots of smaller gifts, too; he wouldn't let her spend a drachma of her own money. She tried to protest at his generosity, but when she did he not only looked affronted but amused, and it was the amusement that made her stop. When he gave her the dress Laurel opened her mouth to object, but then shut it again; it was a shimmering sheath of pale green silk and so beautiful that there was no way she could have refused it.

The luxuriousness of their days together was broken only when Laurel persuaded Niko to take her to an ancient site and they joined the crowds of tourists tramping round the ruins in the sun and heat. She liked Marathon best; there weren't so many visitors there and Niko knew a great deal about the battle. They climbed the mountain to where the signaller with his shining shield to reflect the sun had stood, and looked out over the plain to the great sweeping line of the bay and the clear blue of the sea. 'That's where the Persian fleet was moored,' Niko told her, pointing. 'And that was where the Persians made camp, on the other side of the great marsh. But when the Athenians defeated them they had to try to get back to their ships, and many of them were drowned in the marsh.'

He talked on, graphically describing the battle as if it had happened yesterday. But then he stopped speaking and the place was very silent, very still. Laurel shivered, despite the heat, feeling the spirits of the ancient warriors still haunting the plain. Seeing

it, Niko put his arm round her and held her close
against him. Then he kissed her. His lips were warm,
sensuous, his hands hot as they caressed her bare
arms. The sun beat down on them from a sky of
brilliant blue, their blended shadows thrown sharp and
clear against the white rock. His lips became more
passionate, and Laurel found herself responding
without reserve. Their friendship had become warm
during the last weeks and Niko had kissed her often,
but always she had kept him at a distance. Somehow
today was different; he had brought history alive for
her. There had been pride in his voice as he'd spoken
of his Athenian ancestors. His face was the face of
the statues she had seen in bronze and stone in the
museums, of Adonis and Apollo; proud and arrogant
and beautiful. Laurel was ripe for love, and at that
moment she knew that she had found it with Niko.

That night, after they'd had dinner, they went on
to a night-club where they danced until the small
hours. They drank champagne and ouzo and were very
happy, very close. And this time, when Niko asked
her to stay in Athens, Laurel raised no more objec-
tions. He took her to his apartment, close to the centre
of the city, but high enough to be above the noise of
the traffic. He gave her no time to be shy or to change
her mind, undressing her with swift, experienced
hands and making love to her with all the fervour and
energy of frustrated youth.

At first Laurel was taken aback by the fierceness
of his lovemaking, but then succumbed, over-
whelmed by his passion, and responded to it avidly.
They made love far into the night, and when she told
him that she loved him, Niko huskily murmured that
he loved her too.

After that night there was no question of her returning to Delphi to work on the site, even when her wrist was better. They went back there only once, to collect her things and for Laurel to apologise to the director for deserting him. He looked at her face, radiant with love and happiness, hesitated for a moment, but then immediately forgave her and wished her well.

From then on a great deal of their time seemed to be spent in making love. Even, sometimes, on those deserted beaches, although Laurel could never relax when they did; she was always afraid that someone would see them from the cliffs or from a boat at sea. The long hot summer passed in an idyllic dream. Laurel was head over heels in love with Niko and lived from day to day, never thinking about the future. Occasionally he left her alone for a few hours during the day while he went to his 'office', as he called it, and once Niko had to go to a family party in the evening. He dressed up for it, wearing a dark evening suit, and looked so handsome that he turned Laurel on and he had to tear himself away. But he was back early and was pulling off his clothes almost before he was in the door.

When her wrist was better they spent a couple of weeks sailing round the Cyclades, the group of islands south-east of the mainland. But it was towards the end of those two weeks that Niko began to change. Whenever they landed at an island he would go ashore to phone. 'To check with the office,' he said. At first this didn't make any difference, but one day he came back to the boat, his face dark and moody. Laurel knew at once that something was wrong and waited for him to tell her, but when he didn't she came right out and asked him.

Niko gave her a brooding look. 'My father is back in Athens.'

He didn't explain further, and, even though Laurel felt closer to him than anyone in her life, she felt that he had shut her out and she was reluctant to question him. He'll tell me when he's ready, she thought. But Niko became more moody with every phone call. And now, when he made love to her, there was a kind of frenzy and despair about it. One night as they lay together in the cabin, their bodies satiated and wet with perspiration, he said against her neck, 'You'll be going back to England soon.'

Was that what he was afraid of? Quickly Laurel turned to him and put her hand on his face. 'Not if you don't want me to. If you want me to stay here with you I will.'

'But you have to go back to college, take your degree.'

She gave him a misty smile, her eyes full of tenderness. 'I love you, Niko, darling. I'll do whatever you want.' He stared at her, a strange look in the depths of his eyes. Lifting his hand he caught hers and held it crushingly tight. He seemed about to say something, but Laurel said, 'I want to stay with you now, be with you always. Forever.'

His expression changed and the grip on her hand lessened. 'But I want you to go back and finish your course,' he said shortly. 'You must do that.'

'Must?'

'Yes. You cannot just give up your education. That would be wrong. You would soon hate me if I let you do that.'

'I could never hate you, idiot.' But Laurel smiled at his consideration of her. 'All right. But—we will see each other often, won't we?' There was anxiety in her voice.

He hesitated, but then Niko looked into her face and smiled. 'Of course.' He bent to kiss her lightly on the lips. 'During the holidays. Whenever I can get to England.' His eyes lightened. 'After all, we have plenty of time. And time is what we need.'

She frowned, but then, intuitively, Laurel understood and said, 'To convince your father, you mean?'

Niko gave a rueful grin. 'Yes. He might be more willing to accept a professor of classics than a student.'

'Does it really matter?'

'To me, no,' he said with a sudden flare of passion. 'But to my father...' He sighed heavily, immediately dismal again. 'He thinks I'm far too young and irresponsible to settle down. And when I do he wants me to marry a Greek girl—a daughter of one of his business friends.'

'He has someone picked out for you?' Laurel asked in fear.

'No. Any daughter will do,' Niko said bitterly.

She gave a sigh of relief. 'That's all right, then. All you have to do is to convince him that you love me and can't possibly marry anyone else,' Laurel said with all the confidence and optimism of youth. 'That won't be so hard, will it? Will it?' she said again as she kissed him, her body moving sensuously against his. 'Promise me you'll try.'

He groaned and promised, but two days later they sailed back to Piraeus and the next day Niko drove Laurel to Athens and put her on a plane for London.

England was cold and wet, a whole universe away from the sun-soaked beaches of Greece. Her parents were angry because she'd stayed away longer than she'd intended and so hadn't been home to look after the pets while they went on their own holiday. And Laurel missed Niko terribly; they had been together for nearly two months and she had got used to having him dote on her, and always being with her. She had got used, too, to being escorted to all the best places, to having waiters and doormen rushing to serve them, to living at a high level. And, after a few days, her body began to ache with need of him.

She told him so when he phoned her, as he did almost every day. They were the equivalent of love letters, those phone calls, but who wanted to go to the bother of writing when they could say so much more, hear all the soft intimate nuances, over the phone?

When Laurel went back to college it wasn't so easy; there were societies she had to attend, and the other girls in the house she shared got annoyed when she hogged the phone most evenings. They had started to make tentative plans to see each other at Christmas, but one night towards the end of October Laurel made sure she was alone when she took Niko's call and answered him only in nervous monosyllables.

'Laurel? Are you all right? You sound different.'

'No, I'm the same. At least, no, I'm not. I'm afraid I'm not. Oh, Niko, I . . . Something's happened. I mean it hasn't happened and I——'

'Laurel, what is it?'

Her throat constricted, Laurel stammered, 'I—I think I'm pregnant.'

The silence at the other end of the line was shattering in its suddenness. Then Niko said slowly, 'Are you sure?'

'As sure as I can be. I bought one of those test kits and it was—it was positive. Oh, Niko, what are we going to do? I wish you were here. I need you.'

'Don't worry about it,' he said quickly. 'You must go to the university clinic and they'll arrange for you to have an abortion. If it costs anything let me know and I'll send you the money. Laurel? Laurel, are you there?'

It was a long moment before she answered. 'Yes, I'm still here.'

'Did you hear what I said?'

'Yes, I heard you.' Her voice rose. 'I wish I hadn't heard you. Niko, this is our baby we're talking about. A human being. Our child. A child of our wonderful lovemaking, of that wonderful summer. How can you just talk about getting rid of it as if it's a piece of rubbish? *How can you?*'

'Laurel, we have to be practical. We——'

But she burst out, 'Practical! Don't you have any feelings for it? None at all?'

'Listen to me. You're upset, that's natural.' His voice grew soothing. 'Think what it would do to us, to you. You wouldn't be able to finish your course. And my father...' He broke off.

'What the hell has it got to do with your father, Niko? This is between you and me.'

'You don't understand,' he said shortly. 'My father would never agree.' His tone hardened. 'You've got to have an abortion, Laurel.'

'No, I can't. It's murder.'

He tried to argue with her but she wouldn't listen and grew hysterical. In the end Niko said sharply, 'Laurel, stop crying and listen. I will fly over to see you tomorrow and we'll work this out. You must tell me where to meet you.'

Laurel gave a hiccuping sob, but managed to pull herself together a little, heartened by the knowledge that she would soon see him. They agreed that Laurel would hire a car and meet him at the airport. 'But what if you can't get a flight?' she questioned anxiously.

'Don't worry; I'll use the family plane,' Niko said tersely.

When she saw him the next day Laurel was so overcome by emotion that she could hardly speak. She clung to him, tears of relief in her eyes, sure now that everything would be OK. 'Oh, Niko, I've missed you so much.'

He kissed her quickly, almost perfunctorily, but then held her away from him, glancing uneasily round the crowded concourse. 'Let's get out of here.' Putting a hand under her elbow, Niko walked her quickly out of the airport, his hand raised to his face as if he found the light too much even though he was wearing dark glasses. In the car he sat hunched down in his seat, his coat collar up, and didn't sit normally until they had turned off the main road and were out in open country.

Laurel drove to a stretch of woodland, a local beauty spot that was full of people on summer weekends, but was empty on this chill autumn day, and down a track that took them well out of sight of the road. She turned off the engine then and went into his arms. Niko held her, kissed her properly, and for a few wonderful minutes it was as it had been in Greece, but then Niko drew back, his face bleak.

'I'm so glad you came,' Laurel said quickly before he could speak. 'And I'm sorry this has happened. I didn't *want* it to happen, of course, but now that it has...' She reached up and took off his glasses, then gave him a searching look. 'Aren't you at all pleased, Niko? I thought Greek men liked children.'

'Of course I like children. But not now, Laurel. I told you that I needed time to bring my father round to accept you. Can't you see that this will only make him think I'm even more irresponsible?'

'Well, prove to him that you're not. Show him that you're willing to take on marriage and fatherhood. Surely he'll have to respect you if you do that?'

'You don't know him. He'll never allow it.' Niko's lower lip thrust forward moodily and his eyes were bleak.

'Just how old are you, Niko?' Laurel said angrily. 'I thought you were old enough to make your own decisions, not have to ask your father's permission.'

He swung round on her, his voice harsh. 'Don't try to coerce me, Laurel. In Greece it is different; you have to obey the head of the family.'

'And what about me?' she demanded fiercely. 'Don't I count for anything? And what about our baby?'

'You will have to have an abortion,' he answered without hesitation.

'Well, I won't.'

'Is it against your religion?'

'No, it's against my belief in humanity,' she shot back.

He stared at her, frowning, his face grim as he recognised her implacable determination. Niko desperately set out to persuade and cajole her then, giving a hundred reasons why it was all wrong, but, although Laurel listened to him, her green eyes stayed unblinkingly on his face. He broke off eventually, unable to go on beneath the growing sadness and scorn in her gaze. Humiliated by it, he became angry. 'You're taking away any chance we had by your stubbornness. You're a little fool!' He swung away from her and put his head in his hands.

Reaching out, Laurel put her hands on the steering-wheel and gripped it tightly. 'I want my child's father to be a man who can stand up for himself, not a boy at his father's beck and call. If you can't do that, Niko, then maybe it would be better if you just went back to Greece and we never saw each other again.'

'And leave you to manage on your own! No, I won't do that.' He struck the dashboard with his clenched fist and muttered fiercely under his breath, Greek words that she didn't understand. He straightened and raised his chin. 'I will take care of you,' he said grimly, but with arrogant pride back in his face.

'You will?' She lifted shining eyes to his.

'Yes. I will go back to Athens and I will see my father. I will tell him that I love you and want to marry you. And if he says no, then I will say to hell with him.'

'Oh, wow!' Laurel laughed in relieved, excited happiness. 'And then you'll come back for me? Oh, Niko, it's going to be wonderful.'

'Yes. Yes, it will be wonderful.' He gave her a big hug. 'It is time I stopped taking orders and started to live my own life.' He gave an excited shout of laughter.

'We will manage, somehow we will manage. Maybe I come to live in England.' In his rebellious delight his English slipped a little. 'And we will be happy, will we not? You and I and the little one. I will build my own empire. My great-grandfather started with nothing and so can I. I'll show him that I don't need him or his money.'

Laurel was too relieved and happy to really take in what he was saying. 'I'll have to tell my parents,' she was saying. 'They'll like you, I know they will. And you're sure to like them. And we can get married in the village church. Nothing too elaborate, of course.'

On a high of exhilaration, Niko dragged himself away from his own thoughts to hug her and say, 'Your father; he will not take his gun to me?'

They both burst into laughter at the thought, then kissed rapturously. For another hour they made wonderful, unbelievably impractical plans for the future. They would find a flat; Niko would start his empire from it and they would share looking after the baby until Laurel finished her course. Everything would turn out marvellously and they were going to be incredibly happy.

Niko was eager to get back and face his father, so that they could start their new life. 'I'll come back the day after tomorrow,' he promised. 'Don't come to the airport; I'll come to your digs. But don't go to college that day; I want to spend it with you.'

'All right. I'll make sure we're alone. Goodbye, my darling.' They kissed passionately in the car and then Niko tore himself away, striding openly, head held high, into the airport that he had left so furtively.

Laurel was naturally a tidy person, but she spent all her spare time the next day cleaning out not only

her room but all the shared rooms of the house as
well. She sang as she worked, her heart full to bursting
with happiness. She was too excited to sleep much
that night and was up early the next morning to go
out to buy food for a delicious dinner that she intended to cook for Niko that night. He hadn't been
able to specify any time, but she thought the earliest
he could be there was about eleven o'clock. She waited
eagerly, not even putting on the radio in case he should
call her and she didn't hear the phone ring. Lunchtime
came and Laurel was too excited to eat and went to
lean on the windowsill that looked out over the street,
her eyes searching for him in every car that came
along.

By three Laurel was becoming impatient. Several
times she went to the phone, tempted to call Niko's
number in Athens; but he wouldn't be there, of
course, he would be on his way, perhaps be suffering
a delay somewhere along the line. Maybe he'd had to
get a scheduled flight, she thought. If he'd had a row
with his father then the family plane would no longer
be available to him. But if that was so surely he would
have called to tell her?

Her stomach began to protest noisily, and Laurel
remembered that she was eating for two—and one of
them was hungry even if she wasn't. Going to the
kitchen, she began to make herself a sandwich, finding
a sudden craving for sultanas and honey. Must have
been all that Greek sunshine, she thought with a happy
grin.

Suddenly finding her appetite, Laurel went to take
her first bite when the doorbell rang. Dropping the
sandwich, she ran out into the hall and flung the door
open. 'Niko, at last! We'll have hardly any time to

make love before——' She stopped abruptly. The man standing on the doorstep was not only older than Niko but much taller and with very fair hair.

'Oh, sorry.' She blushed. 'I was expecting someone else.'

'Nikolaos Alexiakis?'

'Why—why, yes.' Her eyes widened in surprise.

'Then you must be Miss Laurel Marland.'

'Yes. Who are you?'

'My name is Ross Ashton. I represent the British interests of the Alexiakis family. May I come in?' He stepped forward as he spoke, giving her no time to protest, and closed the door behind him.

For a few minutes they stood in the hall, Ross Ashton's cold grey eyes going over her assessingly. Then Laurel said jerkily, 'Where's Niko? Has—has something happened to him?'

'He won't be coming,' the man told her. His eyes came up to meet the growing shock in hers, and there was cruel finality in his voice as he added, 'Not now. Not ever.'

CHAPTER TWO

'I DON'T—I don't believe you.' Somehow Laurel got the words out.

'It's quite true.' The glance that Ross Ashton swept over her was little short of contemptuous. 'He has asked me to inform you that your sordid little attempt to blackmail him into marriage has failed and that he never wants to see you again.'

She stared at him, not believing her own ears, then got suddenly angry. 'Niko would never say that! He wouldn't be so cruel. It's his father who has sent you. You're trying to trick me.' She turned to reach for the door latch. 'Get out of here. Go on, get out!'

But he put his arm out and stopped her before she could get the door open. 'If Niko had wanted to come why isn't he here instead of me?'

'Because something must have been done to prevent him. He promised to be here. And he loves me; he would have come if he could,' she said with complete conviction, her voice high with anger.

Ross Ashton's eyes narrowed and he frowned. 'He won't be coming, Miss Marland. I can assure you of that.' He hesitated for a moment, then said coldly, 'He belongs in Greece, with his family. He is the heir to his father's business interests. But then you already know that.'

Laurel nodded helplessly. 'Yes, he told me that his father wanted him to take over the family business. But he said if his father didn't agree he'd give it all up and come here to be with me.' She shook her head wordlessly, still not taking it in. 'He wouldn't do this to me. He loves me. We love each other,' she burst out. Lifting her head she looked at the tall, with-drawn man in front of her, her eyes desperately pleading, but he merely shrugged expressively.

It was that shrug, as if she was just a trivial nuisance, that finally convinced Laurel that he meant what he said. 'No. No!' She felt as if she'd just been told that Niko was dead. The world began to whirl around her and she slumped back against the wall. Ashton put his hand out to support her but she tore herself free, unable to bear his touch, and ran, reeling from side to side, up to her room, where she slammed the door shut behind her and collapsed on to the bed.

She was crying so much that she didn't hear him follow her into her room a few minutes later. He touched her on the shoulder, startling her, and said, 'Here, drink this.'

He was holding a cup of coffee out to her, strong and hot by the look of it. Did he really think that was going to help? With a flare of pure rage Laurel hit out at his arm, sending the coffee flying. Most of it went over him, making him gasp aloud as the scalding liquid soaked through his trousers. Quickly Ashton turned and strode away, and Laurel heard the taps in the bathroom running. Serve him damn well right, she thought. He didn't have to *enjoy* being Niko's messenger boy. No, not Niko's, his father's. Left to himself, Niko would never have let her down like this. He had been ready to give up everything to marry her. His father must have bullied and coerced him, but if she could only talk to Niko, boost up his courage again . . . Filled with sudden hope, Laurel swung off the bed and ran downstairs to the phone. First she tried Niko's flat but there was no reply, so instead she got hold of the operator and said, 'I want a person-to-person call to Mr Nikolaos Alexiakis.' She gave her name and the number of Niko's office, adding, 'It's very urgent, please.'

She waited impatiently for what seemed an endless time, gripping the phone tightly to her ear, alert for any sound. At length the international operator came back to her. 'I'm sorry, I'm unable to connect you to the person you require.'

'You mean he's not there?'

'I'm unable to connect you,' the operator repeated.

'Please try again,' Laurel said desperately. 'Tell him it's terribly important I speak to him.'

'Very well; just one moment, please.'

'You're wasting your time.'

Ross Ashton's voice behind her made her swing round. He was coming down the stairs, his trousers stain-free and completely dry. He must have rinsed them and dried them with one of the hairdriers in the bathroom, Laurel realised with the small particle of her mind that wasn't crying out for Niko to hurry up and answer the phone. She turned away again, uninterested in him.

'I'm sorry, I'm still unable to connect you.' The operator's voice came clearly over the line.

'But you *must* be able to. I have to speak to him! Keep trying. Tell him——'

'I've already told him who you are,' the operator cut in unsympathetically. 'But he refuses to take your call.'

'But that can't be true. Are you sure it was him?'

'Quite sure. The gentleman identified himself.'

'But he must speak to me. He must!' Laurel's voice began to rise hysterically. 'Look, just put me through to the number and I'll speak to him myself. I——'

A man's hand reached forward and cut her off. Enraged, Laurel turned on Ashton and tried to hit him with the receiver. But he was ready for her this time and caught hold of it, wrenching it from her hand. Then he grabbed hold of her wrists so that she couldn't let fly at him, warily holding her at arm's length so that she couldn't kick him either. Not that it occurred to her to try. For a few moments Laurel struggled against his hold, but he was far too strong for her, gripping her wrists so tightly that he hurt her. Suddenly her strength seemed to drain away and she slumped in his hold. For a couple of minutes he continued to take her weight, suspecting some trick, but then Ross let her go and she fell to her knees.

'Come and sit down,' he said shortly, and half carried her to an armchair. Putting his hands on his hips, Ross Ashton stood looking frowningly down at her.

Laurel leaned back against the chair, her face devoid of colour, her hands balled into tight fists as she struggled to control herself, struggled to accept what had happened. Lifting pain-racked eyes, she said dully, 'Go away. Go away and leave me alone.'

'I haven't yet completed all I was sent to do.'

Her heart froze as she stared at him. 'You mean—there's more?'

His voice devoid of any emotion, Ross said, 'I'm instructed to tell you that if you insist on having the child, so long as you produce a doctor's certificate to prove that you really are pregnant, then an allowance will be provided for you until the baby is born. The child will then have to have a blood test to prove beyond all doubt that Niko is definitely the father. If that is conclusive then the allowance will be increased to a level where you will be able to live comfortably until the child is eighteen. You will, of course, be required to sign an affidavit promising to make no further demands on Niko and also swearing that you will never attempt to see him again or to force your child on him at any time in the future.'

Coming to an end, Ross gave her a wary look, half expecting her to hit out at him again, but Laurel's face had turned to stone as she sat and stared at him.

When she didn't speak, Ross said, 'The allowance would be an adequate one, enough for you to hire someone to look after the child while you finish your studies.' Still Laurel didn't answer, and he said, 'I take it that you agree to this arrangement, then?'

A long shudder ran through her. 'Are you a lawyer?' Laurel asked dully.

'Yes, I am.'

'I thought you must be.' Her green eyes held his, scorching them with her scorn. 'You so obviously enjoy doing other people's dirty work!'

He flinched and his jaw tightened, but Ross said shortly, 'Will you accept Niko's offer?'

'No,' Laurel retorted, anger bringing life back into her brain. 'Tell him to go to hell.'

'He'll never marry you, if that's what you're still angling for. His father would disown him.'

'I didn't want his father; I wanted him,' Laurel shot back.

'But presumably you wouldn't have been averse to Niko's inheriting his father's shipping line, or his property in Athens, or his private island, or his other business interests? Something like a billion pounds' worth,' Ross returned with biting sarcasm.

She gazed at him in open-mouthed amazement. Her voice shaking, Laurel said, 'What—what did you say?'

'It's too late to play the innocent,' he said curtly. 'You knew all this even before you started going out with Niko.'

She shook her head in bewilderment. 'But I didn't. We knew each other at university. And then I was working in Greece and sprained my wrist, and got so bored that I looked him up.'

'How convenient,' Ross sneered, in complete disbelief.

Laurel wasn't used to being so openly insulted. For a moment she was too taken aback by it to react, but then humiliation brought anger again and she somehow dragged herself to her feet and found the strength to face him, her head held high. 'I don't care what you think. After all, you're only a messenger boy. But I loved Niko and I was willing to give up an education and a possible career that means a great deal to me for him,' she said with raw dignity. 'But it seems he doesn't have the courage to give up anything for me. Well, all right, that's his choice. But it doesn't give you the right to come here and insult me.' Her chin came up even higher and her voice grew stronger. 'You can go back to him and tell him that I don't want his money and I no longer want him. There's no way I want a coward for a husband.'

A strange look had come into Ross's eyes, and it was a moment before he said, 'You would be foolish not to accept the offer.'

Laurel shook her head. 'No. Niko is the loser in this, not me.' She gestured towards the door. 'Will you go now, please?'

'But I——'

Her eyes flashed daggers of green ice at him. 'You've done what you've been sent to do; now get out. Go back and report to your master. Tell Niko's father that he doesn't have to worry; that I wouldn't *lower* myself ever to try and contact him again.'

Ross's face was set, the strange look in his eyes deeper now. He seemed to be preoccupied, but after a few moments he blinked, as if dragging his thoughts back to the present. 'All right, if that's what you want.' He took a card from his pocket. 'But you'd better have this in case you change your mind. You can get in touch with me at any time.'

'I won't,' Laurel said firmly.

'Nevertheless.' Ross's mouth twisted and he gave a short laugh that seemed strangely bitter.

He gave her a quick glance, but she had turned her face away. 'Yes, of course.' But he put the card down on the table before turning to go.

When he reached the door, Laurel, not looking at him, said, 'I'm sorry about the coffee. I hope you weren't—hurt.'

He paused with his hand on the knob and turned to look back at her, standing tall and proud, determined not to let him see her hurt, her thick mane of red hair and the delicate outline of her face framed by the autumn sunlight from the window. His voice curt and bitter again, he said, 'Isn't it always the messenger who receives the punishment?'

Puzzled, Laurel slowly turned her head to look at him, but Ross had already gone. She heard the front door shut firmly behind him, and then she was left alone in the empty, silent house, a silence broken by her desperate cry of anguish as she let unhappiness and despair wash over her at last.

It was a few weeks before Laurel found the courage to go home and tell her parents what had happened. There was no fear of their advising her to have an abortion; they had passed on to her their own feelings about human rights. They were of course upset and disappointed that she had let herself become pregnant. 'Surely in this day and age you could have avoided it?' her father said in some anger. 'And what about the man? Is he a fellow student?'

'It was while I was on holiday,' Laurel told them. 'And I've lost touch with him. I don't know where he is. It was just a—a holiday romance, that's all. Nothing special.' It hurt to describe her love for Niko in those terms and it made her parents even angrier that she had had so little self-regard, but it was better than laying bare the truth. Anything was better than having to discuss it all, to tell them that Niko was too weak to stand up to his own father.

But after they'd got over their first shock, her father became practical. 'Well, whatever happens you mustn't let it interfere with your education; that's the most important thing at the moment. We've sacrificed a great deal so that you could go to university, you know.'

'Yes, I know, Dad. I'm sorry.'

His voice hardened. 'After it's born you'll have to let the baby go for adoption.'

Laurel's face whitened. 'Adoption?'

'Well, there's no way you'll be able to keep it yourself,' he pointed out. 'Not if you want to stay on at university to take a doctorate degree.'

'But I can't just give the baby away, not know what's happened to it,' Laurel said in horror.

Her father looked as if he was going to argue, but Laurel's mother, her voice excited, said quickly, 'Maybe there's a way round this that will be good for everyone. Alec and Georgina have been trying for a baby for ages,' she explained, naming Laurel's elder brother and his wife. 'But they haven't been lucky, and Georgina told me only a few weeks ago that they're seriously starting to think about adopting a child. Well, why don't they adopt Laurel's baby? That way she'll get to see it and will know that it's being well looked after. Laurel will be able to finish her education and Alec and Georgina won't have to go through years of waiting for a suitable child to come up for adoption.'

They talked the idea over for a while, but there was little point. It was obviously an ideal solution to the problem. To her mother it was almost a fortuitous coincidence, especially as Alec, her first-born, was her favourite child. As soon as Laurel had said yes, she rushed to phone him and tell him the news, and that night the excited couple came round and everything was settled. They talked about it so happily that Laurel almost felt superfluous, like a surrogate mother, as if her feelings for the child didn't matter at all. But that was unfair; as her mother had said, this way she would always know her child, even though it would think of her as an aunt.

For the next few months Laurel threw herself into her work, studying hard and rarely going out socially.

During the Christmas holidays the other girls in her digs went skiing together, but Laurel went home. It wasn't an enjoyable holiday; Georgina was forever asking her how she was and insisting that she go for check-ups and scans. And her sister-in-law was eagerly buying baby clothes while her mother was making a beautifully worked pram quilt. The two women chatted eagerly about the baby, making plans, discussing possible names, but would hastily stop when Laurel walked into the room, although sometimes, when she was sitting in the window-seat, reading, they would forget that she was there and go on talking.

Most of the time Laurel was able to take it all because she knew that it was for the best and that she was lucky that the baby was to be kept in the family, but once she couldn't bear it any more and rounded on them. 'What the hell do you think I am?' she demanded forcefully. 'A brood hen? A baby-making machine? This is *my* baby you're talking about. I'm the one who's having it! Not Georgina. It's growing inside *me*. It's dependent on *me*.' Then, taken aback by her own vehemence, she ran up to her room and shut herself in. Her mother came up a short time later, put her arms round her and comforted her. 'All women get emotional when they're pregnant,' the older woman advised. 'Usually they take it out on their husbands.'

'But I haven't got a husband,' Laurel said bitterly.

'It'll soon be over. Only another few months now. This time next year you'll be able to go skiing with the other girls,' her mother soothed. 'It will be as if it had never happened.'

No, not that, Laurel thought. Because every time she saw the baby she would be reminded of Niko—

and of just how unreliable men could be. But at least it had taught her never to trust a man again. In future she would steer well clear of ever getting involved, and she would make darn sure that her emotions stayed firmly in check. Not for her another love-affair. She was going to work so hard for her degrees that she would pass with honours, and from then on she would concentrate entirely on her career, letting nothing get in its way. Laurel vowed to stay heart-whole for the rest of her life.

In February Ross Ashton came to see her again. He came one cold Saturday morning and was waiting at the house when she got back from shopping. One of the other girls had let him in and was chatting to him in the sitting-room, obviously avid with curiosity as Laurel had never revealed the name of the baby's father. He stood up when Laurel came into the room, his eyes running over her. By now her pregnancy was advanced enough to be obvious, and she resented his inspection.

'Seen enough?' she said rudely.

He had been about to greet her, but instead he raised a sardonic eyebrow. 'How are you?' he asked coolly.

'As well as can be expected in the circumstances. What do you want?'

Aware of the other girl listening with wide-eyed interest, Ross picked up his overcoat from a chair and said, 'Why don't we go out for a walk?' And, stepping forward, he put his hand under Laurel's elbow and firmly led her into the hall. 'Is this your coat? Here, let me help you put it on. And you'll need a scarf, I think.'

Laurel started to protest, but found herself with a thick coat on, a scarf wound round her neck, and being propelled outside into the street. 'Do you mind? It's cold out here,' she said indignantly.

'Then we'll go somewhere and have a coffee.' He walked her the few paces to a sleekly expensive car and held the door open for her.

'But I don't want to go anywhere with you,' she objected.

'All right, then we'll talk here on the street, in the cold.'

'I have nothing to talk to you about, either.' Ross didn't say anything, just looked at her. For a few moments Laurel returned his gaze angrily, but then she dropped her eyes and flushed. 'I'm sorry. You—you took me by surprise.'

'That's OK.' His voice was much milder. 'Shall we go and have that coffee now?'

Reluctantly she got into the car and directed him to a coffee-shop only a half-mile or so away. They went in and found a quiet table, Ross taking her coat from her to hang up. 'This isn't my coat,' she said fretfully, noticing for the first time.

To her surprise he smiled at her as he sat down opposite. 'Sorry.'

She gazed at him, really looking at him, seeing him as a human being for the first time. He raised a quizzical eyebrow, making her quickly look down at the table. Her hands balled into clenched fists, she said, 'How—how's Niko?' forcing the words out.

'The same as ever,' Ross said evenly. He was watching her closely, his mouth a little twisted.

She gave a small, mirthless laugh at that. 'Is he?' She raised vulnerable green eyes and said with mental masochism, 'I take it I'm not the first girl that Niko has got into trouble?'

His brief pause gave her the answer even before Ross said, 'No, you're not. It's happened twice before. But both times the girls agreed to have an abortion.'

'I see.' She looked quickly away again.

'Niko is young and rich, a playboy,' Ross said calmly. 'His father encourages him to—play around, if you like, while he's young, so that he'll be ready to settle down when he's married.'

'It seems to me it would have the opposite effect,' Laurel said scornfully.

'Possibly.' Ross's lip curled in slight amusement.

'Has he—has Niko sent you here?'

'I was asked to find out if you really were pregnant and, if so, to renew the offer of an allowance.'

It was an ambiguous answer, but Laurel chose to believe that Niko had sent him. 'Didn't you tell him that I didn't want his money?'

'The message was passed on, yes. But circumstances might have made you change your mind.'

'I told you I wouldn't.' Her chin came up.

Ross gave her a contemplative look. 'Pride can be expensive,' he observed. 'And in some cases foolish.'

Laurel gave a bitter little smile. 'In some cases it's all one has.'

Ross leaned forward, his manner suddenly forceful. 'The offer still stands, Laurel. Why won't you take it; for the child's sake if not your own? Can you really afford to be proud when it comes to having everything you need for a healthy baby?'

'The baby will be fine,' she said stubbornly. 'I don't need anything.'

His eyes studied her closed face and then he sat back in his seat. The coffee came, strong and frothy, in thick china cups. Stirring his, Ross said, 'What are you going to do when it's born?'

After hesitating a moment, Laurel said shortly, 'That's none of your business.'

'I'm afraid it is.'

'Because you're *paid* to make it your business,' she flashed at him. 'Look, why can't you leave me alone? I told you that's what I wanted.'

'You were extremely upset at the time. Now that you've had time to get over your disappointment and to look at the future clearly, you must see that——'

'Don't tell me what I must or must not do,' she interrupted fiercely. 'I'm fed up with forever being told what's good for me.'

He eyed her narrowly, his grey eyes not unsympathetic. 'Are your family giving you the support you expected?'

'Yes.'

She said it with deep finality, but he wasn't the type who could be frozen out. 'And are you going to keep the child? Bring it up yourself?'

A shadow darkened her eyes, but then Laurel snapped out, 'What the hell does Niko or his father care? It's nothing to do with them—or you.'

Ross frowned, then leaned forward again and said shortly, 'Look, forget Niko, if that's what you want. But you must think of the child. It's hard for a woman bringing up a child on her own; you've no idea how hard. OK, so maybe thousands of girls do it nowadays, but not all of them have your opportunity for a good career. You're highly intelligent, Laurel. If you forgo your future for the sake of this child you'll eventually come to resent it, even though you'll love it at the same time. Isn't it sensible to take the allowance offered to you so that you can have the best of both worlds; your child and a career? And in the long run wouldn't that be best for the child? When you're established in your profession, or if you marry, then you'll be independent enough to say to hell with the allowance, but not now, surely?'

What he said made sense, and Laurel had the feeling that he was going to go on pushing his wretched allowance at her indefinitely if she didn't stop him once and for all. So she said, 'I'm not keeping it. My brother and his wife are going to adopt it.'

'I see.' Ross leaned back in his seat. 'And are you happy with that arrangement?'

'Yes, of course. It will leave me—free to stay on at university, but I'll still be able to see the baby and know that it's all right.'

'It sounds a marvellous solution to the problem,' he remarked.

'Yes, it is.' But a shadow darkened her eyes again, emeralds that had lost a lot of their lustre. Rallying, Laurel said, 'So you see, everything's taken care of and I don't need their money.'

Their eyes met across the table, his searching, Laurel's defiant. 'You're being very brave,' he said shortly.

She shrugged. 'What else is there to be?'

'You really were in love with Niko, weren't you?'

'Yes—not that I expect you to believe it.'

'But I do believe you.'

Laurel opened her mouth to say that she couldn't care less either way, but the words died. Ross, with his tanned, angular features and blond hair, was good-looking enough to have had many women in love with him, she realised, so presumably he recognised it when he saw it. And he was young still, only about thirty, she thought. Young to be the Alexiakis family's representative anyway. And he hadn't been altogether unkind, had tried to help her. 'Thanks,' she said huskily.

He nodded. 'So there's nothing I can do for you?'

'No.'

She expected him to suggest they leave then, but instead he sighed and said, 'There's just one outstanding piece of business, I'm afraid.'

'There is?' She gave him a surprised, wary look.

'Your written agreement not to make any approaches to Niko in the future and not to make any claim on him on behalf of your child.'

Laurel's mouth twisted bitterly and she sent him a look of flashing disdain. 'So *that's* what you really came for. I ought to have known.'

'I'm sorry.'

'You—no, *they*—are beneath contempt. Is Niko's father's own word so false that he can't believe anyone else's?'

'Not all girls are as—honest as you, Laurel.'

'And am I supposed to take that as a compliment?' She was suddenly so angry that it choked her. She wanted to be rid of him, rid of the whole thing. Thrusting out her hand, she said fiercely, 'All right, give me your agreement. You're so efficient that I'm quite sure you've brought it with you,' she added in withering ridicule.

Ross's face hardened grimly, but he reached into his jacket pocket and took out a long envelope. Extracting a document from it, he laid it on the table in front of her. It was about three pages long, she saw. Holding out her hand, she said icily, 'A pen, please. I'm sure you have one of those as well.'

He handed one to her, a slim gold fountain-pen. 'After you've read each page, if you agree with the conditions, then sign it and I'll witness it on the last page.'

But Laurel grabbed the pen from his hand and angrily scrawled her signature on each page without demeaning herself by reading them, then tossed the pen and agreement back at him.

'But you must read it, Laurel,' Ross protested. 'Here, take it back and——'

Getting to her feet, her eyes blazing, she said, 'I'm not damn well interested. I don't care what it says. All I want is for them to leave me alone. You can go back and tell them that. My baby and I are too darn good to want anything to do with wimps like them.' She glowered at him, furious now that she had even thought of him as human. 'And just who the hell said you could call me Laurel? My name is Miss Marland to underlings like you. And if I consider the Alexiakises to be wimps, what the hell does that make you?' Then she grabbed up her things and strode out of the café, not bothering to look behind her, and ran to swing herself on to the first bus that came along.

The baby was due in May, dangerously close to her exams, unfortunately, but everything had been arranged so that Georgina would take over the baby just as soon as Laurel came out of the hospital, a couple of days after the birth, if all went well. As the time grew nearer Laurel found it harder to concentrate on her work. She would put her hand on her stomach, feeling the baby moving energetically, eager for life, and a dreamy look would come into her eyes.

Would it be a boy or a girl? she wondered. Would it
have Niko's thick dark hair or would it be red like
her own? Whichever it was, she knew that it would
be a child of the sun, this baby conceived in the golden
land of Greece. And it ought to know its heritage, be
taken to Greece and taught to speak the language.
But then Laurel remembered that she would have no
say in its upbringing, and teaching the child to speak
Greek of all languages was the last thing that Georgina
would contemplate. They were going to call it Clive
if it was a boy, and Angela if a girl, both of which
Laurel considered to be wimpish names. But then the
child's father and grandfather were wimps, so who
was she to quarrel with a choice that carried on the
tradition? Bitterness filled her heart, but then she
became frustratedly angry. She didn't want her baby
to be called such stupid names, and she didn't want
it to be brought up in the middle-class respectability
that Georgina had all mapped out for it. It ought to
have fun and adventure and . . .

But here Laurel literally took a grip on herself by
digging her nails into her crossed arms; it was nothing
to do with her; she had given up all rights to the baby
when she had agreed to let Georgina and Alex adopt
it. She would see it for a couple of days after it was
born and then they would tactfully take it away while
Laura recovered at home for ten days or so and then
went back to college. 'You must forget you've ever
had it,' her mother had advised her. 'Think of it as
their child.' But that wasn't going to be so easy to do.
As the days passed Laurel grew more morose and
would go for long walks when she should have been
studying. She was drawn to the windows of baby-wear
shops and once or twice couldn't resist buying a

minute garment, then felt stupid and hid it away in a drawer.

Because of these feelings Laurel found it difficult to talk to her mother, so losing the encouragement and reassurance she needed at such a time. She grew nervous and terribly lonely. She wanted someone to talk to; in ordinary circumstances it would have been a husband, but somehow she couldn't see Niko in the role of proud husband and father. Not any more, she thought, her mouth twisting wryly. His weakness, and his treatment of her, had by now largely killed her love for him, but still, deep in her heart, there was and would always be the memory of that perfect summer. And in that memory Niko would always be the young Greek god she had fallen in love with. Neither time nor circumstances could ever change that.

Easter came and went. As her body grew larger Laurel's face became thinner. She wasn't sleeping well and her morale was very low, sometimes making her cry for no real reason—unless being an unmarried, abandoned mother wasn't reason enough. She had none of the radiance women were supposed to get when they were pregnant; she thought she looked terrible, and she felt worse. At times she just wanted to get it all over and done with.

The baby was born two weeks early, so instead of having it at the hospital near to her home, as they had planned, she was whisked into a hospital near her digs. The pains had started in the night so it was one of her flatmates, a fellow student, who went in the ambulance with her and held her hand until ordered away. And then it all happened so quickly that there wasn't really time to be afraid.

It was a boy. And his hair was as dark and thick as Niko's. He was put into Laurel's arms and she stared down at the little crumpled figure that had caused so much consternation and pain. He yawned, as if bored already, but then closed one eye in what was definitely a wink. Laurel laughed—and was hooked for life.

Her girlfriend had loyally been waiting and was finally allowed in to see them. 'Good heavens! Isn't he tiny?' she exclaimed.

They both stared at the baby and he definitely smirked. Just like his father, Laurel thought, a lady-killer already.

'Would you like me to telephone your parents and tell them?'

'No.' Laurel shook her head. 'I'd rather do it myself.'

A nurse came to take the baby from her then and her friend left so that Laurel could get some sleep. But when she woke it was quite a while before she asked if she could use the phone. Her mother answered.

'A boy! Oh, Alec and Georgina will be pleased. And are you all right?'

'Yes, but——'

'Of course you are, you're young and fit.' Her mother said excitedly, 'So your Dad and I are grand-parents at last. How wonderful. What a pity you're so far away, but never mind, I'll phone Georgina and let her know and then we'll all come over this evening so that we can see the baby.'

'Mum——'

'Then, when they let you out, we'll bring you home and they can take the baby.'

'Mum——'

'In a way it's lucky that it's early because it's not so close to your exams. You'll have a bit more time to recover before——'

'*Mum, will you please listen to me?*' Laurel broke through her mother's excited cascade of words. 'If you and Dad want to come and see the baby, fine— but please don't bring Alec and Georgina.'

'But whyever not? Don't you want to see Georgina with it, is that it?'

'No, it . . .' She hesitated, but only to find the right words, and Laurel's voice was firm as she said, 'Mum, I'm sorry, but I'm going to keep the baby. During the last months I've been feeling more and more that I made the wrong decision, and now that I've seen the baby I know that I can't give him up.'

'But you can't! You promised.' Her mother's voice was sharp with disbelief.

'I'm sorry to let you down, but I've made up my mind.'

Her mother started to argue but luckily Laurel's money ran out, so she was able to give a thankful sigh and put down the phone. But she knew they wouldn't leave it there and wasn't at all surprised when they all four turned up that evening, their faces set and angry, determined to have their way. Laurel's heart sank as they pulled the curtains to screen off her bed, but she resisted all their persuasions, arguments and, in the end, threats, apologising profusely, but pointing out that she had been upset when she had agreed to the adoption.

'And what are you now?' her brother demanded. 'It's just post-natal euphoria. In a couple of days you'll probably be feeling depressed and won't be able to wait to give it away.'

'The "it" you're referring to happens to be my son,' Laurel said shortly. 'And maybe in a few days I will be depressed, but it won't make any difference; I'll still want to keep him.'

'And just how do you expect to look after him and still go to university?' her father questioned sharply. 'Don't expect your mother and me to look after him.'

'I don't. Obviously I can't do both, so I'll have to give up university and get a job.'

It was this that made her father really explode, and Laurel couldn't blame him. He let her, and the whole ward, know what he thought about her morals, her family loyalty and her stupidity, among other things, and rounded it off by saying that he washed his hands of her, before stalking out of the ward.

'Now look what you've done!' her mother exclaimed, and burst into tears.

Then it was Georgina's turn to start crying. 'How could you do this to us? We've told everyone that we're adopting a baby. It could be years before we get another chance.'

Putting his arms round his wife, Alec said curtly, 'I'm never going to forgive you for this, Laurel. And don't expect us to help you. If you insist on keeping the baby, then you'll have to do it alone.'

'I didn't expect anything else.'

He stood up. 'Come on, darling. Come on, Mum. We obviously don't matter to Laurel, so let's leave her to get on with it.'

'But we haven't seen the baby yet,' her mother protested.

But Alec put his hand under her arm and marched them both towards the double doors at the end of the ward. Her mother hung back, half turned, and Laurel thought that she was going to resist and come back, but in the end she allowed her son to lead her away.

So it was over. Laurel leant against the pillows feeling drained, but into her veins gradually crept a sense of exhilaration. She was free. No, *they* were free. She would never be just one person ever again, the baby would always be a part of her, no matter what. And now she could choose a name for him—and it definitely wouldn't be Clive.

Some of her university friends came to visit her the following day and her brother phoned to ask her if she'd changed her mind, but when Laurel said no he immediately hung up on her.

It had been fun while her friends were there and they had brought her small gifts, all they could afford when it was so near the end of term. After they'd gone Laurel slept until it was time to eat and for evening visiting time. The babies who were more than a day old were brought round to be put in cots beside their mothers' beds, and then the doors were opened as the visitors, husbands and grandparents mostly, came eagerly in. Laurel sat alone, trying not to watch them all, trying not to feel sad. Picking up a book, she determined to concentrate on it.

A man walked into the ward, good-looking, smartly dressed, very tanned and fit. He paused for a moment in the doorway, looking round, and there was a slight lull in the conversation around the beds as people noticed him and were arrested by his self-confident manner. He was carrying a large basket containing the most beautiful arrangement of pale yellow and cream roses. His eyes swept round the ward and then he strode towards Laurel's bed where she sat looking delicate and fragile, her eyes dark-shadowed, her hair tied back to reveal the long column of her neck. She glanced up as she heard his footsteps, and then stared.

'Hello, Laurel.' Ross Ashton stood looking quizzically down at her. 'Or must I say Miss Marland?'

She felt a silly lump in her throat. 'Laurel will do,' she said huskily.

He put the flowers on the table beside her bed and sat down. 'Congratulations.'

'How did you know?'

'I've been keeping an eye on you.'

He said it rather warily, as if expecting her to be angry, but Laurel found that she had the maturity now not to feel at all resentful. 'Then you know that it's a boy.'

He nodded, but didn't attempt to look at the baby. 'And how are you? Recovering?'

She smiled. 'Yes, I suppose so.'

His eyes widened a little. 'You must be if you can smile. I'm glad you're feeling happy again.'

There was sincerity in his tone, making Laurel realise that she had never had anything to smile about before when he was around. He had brought only unhappiness and bitterness with him. The thought made her suddenly afraid. 'Why have you come?' she asked sharply.

'To bring you some flowers.'

'But what's the real reason?' she said on an acid note. 'Another affidavit for me to sign?'

His jaw tightened a little, but Ross said, 'I suppose I deserved that. No, I merely came to make sure that you and the baby are well. Nothing more.'

'Did—did Niko send you? Did he ask you to keep an eye on me?'

Slowly he shook his head. 'No, sorry. I came of my own accord.'

'I see.' Well, what the hell else had she expected? For Ross to have come at all was obviously beyond the call of duty. Straightening her shoulders, Laurel said proudly, 'That was very kind of you. As you see, we're both fine. You can—you can look at the baby, if you like.'

'Thank you.' He said it gravely, then walked round to the other side of the bed to look down into the cot. Putting out a long-fingered hand, he very gently lowered the blanket a little so that he could fully see the baby's face. Then he gave a small smile. 'He looks just like Niko did when he was born. A miniature version of him.'

'You've known him that long?' Laurel said in surprise.

'All his life.' Ross came to sit beside her again. 'Your brother and his wife must be very excited. When are they coming for the baby?'

'We're leaving tomorrow,' Laurel said diplomatically.

'And what is his name going to be?'

'They want to call him Clive.'

Ross found no comment to make about that. 'And you're still happy with the arrangement?'

'I'm happy that the baby will have the future that's best for him, yes.'

'Good.'

'So you'll have no need to keep an eye on me any more, will you?'

Ross looked amused. He hesitated for a moment, but then said, 'I know you have reason to feel antagonistic towards me, Laurel, but I have great admiration for the way you've handled all this. Very few girls would have stuck so loyally to your principles, and even fewer would have turned down the offer of an allowance.'

He paused and she said an embarrassed, 'Thank you,' thinking that that was what he expected.

But then he said, 'I wonder, when you're feeling better, perhaps after your exams are over, whether we might get together some time? Perhaps go to a concert and then have dinner. Maybe then we could talk like two ordinary people instead of enemies,' he added, raising a quizzical eyebrow.

Surprise kept her silent for a moment. She looked at him and realised the idea wasn't unattractive, but then a great fear that he might find out that she was keeping the baby filled Laurel's mind. He might tell Niko's father and they would try to interfere in her life once more. He began to speak again, but, fear heightening her voice, she said sharply, 'No!' leaving him in no doubt of her feelings.

Ross broke off abruptly, his face setting.

'I'm sorry,' Laurel said quickly, 'but after today I really don't want ever to see you again. I want to start my life all over again and I don't want any reminders of this—this incident. To me you'll always be Mr Alexiakis's lawyer. Surely you can understand that?' She paused for a moment but, before he had time to speak, went on, 'It was kind of you to bring the flowers, but I'm all right, really. I just want to forget all this.'

He nodded and stood up. His mouth twisting with irony, Ross said, 'Well, at least you didn't call me their messenger boy this time.' His grey eyes lingered on her and she thought she saw disappointment in their depths. 'So it's goodbye, then.' She nodded without speaking, and he gave a curt nod. 'I wish you well for the future.' Then he turned and walked away without looking back.

Laurel watched him go, still surprised and her feelings rather confused, but after a few moments she dismissed Ross from her thoughts, turning instead to pick up by far the most important male in her life. Giving her son a look of overwhelming love and tenderness, she said, 'Come here, Troy Marland.'

CHAPTER THREE

'SHIPPING TYCOON'S SON KILLED.' Laurel actually noticed the headline in the paper as she was glancing through it, but the item was on an inside page and she was in a hurry, so she didn't get round to reading any further. Turning to look out of the rain-splashed window of the bus, she saw that she was near her stop, so she folded the paper and pushed her way to the platform. Jumping off as the bus slowed, she strode quickly along the pavements, a tall figure in a belted raincoat, her hair covered by a mannish hat, a big, squashy bag swinging from her shoulder. She reached the gates of the nursery school just as the children began to come out to the waiting mothers, supervised by one of the teachers.

Some of the children were still inside, peering through the windows for mothers who hadn't yet arrived, Troy among them. Some of them had anxious frowns on their little faces, but not Troy; he knew she would always be there. Laurel waved to him, but he had already seen her and was on his way out.

'Hi.' She greeted him with a hug, but he was eager to show her his latest drawing, his name proudly scrawled across the bottom of the sheet. 'What have you drawn today?'

It was a picture of a farmyard with identifiable horses, pigs and cows, and—as always—a brilliantly coloured sun shone in the sky. Laurel smiled to herself, thinking what a true child of the sun he was. 'I should

have called you Apollo,' she told him as she carefully
rolled the drawing and put it away in her bag so that
it wouldn't get wet.

'Who's Pollo?'

'Not Pollo, Apollo. You know who he is. He's the
Greek god of the sun. Don't you remember? I showed
you pictures of his shrine at Delphi in the picture
book.'

She took his hand and they walked to catch the
bus, but their progress was slower because he liked to
look in the shop windows. They chatted together as
they walked, holding a conversation that should have
been in advance of his years, but when the only person
you had to talk to was a child that child soon learned
a large vocabulary. And in Troy's case he had learnt
to speak Greek at the same time as English, so they
used both languages. Laurel had learnt classical Greek
at college, of course, and had found it quite easy to
pick up modern Greek when she was at Delphi and
with Niko. Since then she had made a point of learning
the language fluently through taped lessons, and
working for a Greek family for a couple of years had
helped a great deal. This knowledge Laurel had passed
on to her son so that he was almost bilingual.

It was her big ambition to take Troy to Greece for
a holiday and she was saving hard to do so, but
whenever she got a little money together and had actually begun to plan the holiday, something would
come up—an extra-large bill or the need to move on
again and pay rent in advance—so that her scraped-
together hoard would disappear as if it had never
been.

Life had been extremely hard since Troy was born
almost four and a half years ago, but they were

reasonably settled now and once he went to school full time Laurel hoped to be able to get a better job so that they could have a place of their own. At the moment she was working as a housekeeper-cum-maid-cum-chauffeur-cum secretary-cum everything-else for a family in Hampstead. The father was an architect, the mother a freelance journalist, and they had four young children and a mother-in-law. All of them were extremely disorganised and untidy so that most of the time Laurel felt as if there were seven children she was looking after. In return for working most hours of the day, Laurel was given two basement rooms for herself and Troy, their keep, one whole day and a half-day off each week—which she was seldom free to take—plus a very modest wage. It wasn't the first of such jobs that Laurel had been forced to take; it was difficult to find anything else when you had a small child, but at least with this one there were no grown-up sons or jealous teenage daughters to make life difficult, and the husband hadn't yet made a pass at her. Most men seemed to think that because she was an unmarried mother she must therefore be an easy lay, and that mistaken assumption had led to her abruptly packing their bags and leaving more than one job.

They came to a toy shop, its window hung with gay Christmas lights, and Troy was immediately absorbed in the model cars, as keen on motors as his father had been, but after a few minutes she had regretfully pulled him away. 'We have to get the bus. They're home for lunch today.'

He came obediently, used by now to having his life governed by the whims of employers. When they reached the house Laurel went straight to the kitchen, pushing food that she'd already prepared into the

microwave to heat up even before she had taken off
her coat. Only when the family had been served did
she have time to prepare some lunch for herself and
Troy. When they'd eaten he sat at the table with a
colouring-book while Laurel loaded the washing-
machine and then tackled a great pile of ironing that
had been yesterday's washing. It was a boring job,
but she didn't mind because it gave her a chance to
chat with Troy in Greek, to make him use the language as he described his morning at nursery school.

At three-fifteen she had to put on their coats and
go and meet the children of the family from school,
taking the big estate car this time—they wouldn't have
dreamed of letting their children walk home in the
rain or the petrol fumes from the traffic-choked
streets. When they got back she was expected to
supervise the children while they did their homework
at the kitchen table, and prepare a meal for them and
dinner for the adults, all at the same time. Troy ate
with the children, but Laurel was usually too busy
and ate on her feet, and after dinner was cleared away
she had to put the children to bed and then baby-sit
while she finished the ironing and did any mending
that needed to be done. Often, too, the mother-in-law
would want some typing done for one of the charities
she worked for; she was really generous with her offers
to do 'a little clerical work', all of which ended up on
Laurel's kitchen table. So it was usually gone mid-
night when she crawled into bed, trying not to wake
Troy, who slept in the other single bed in the same
room. The other room Laurel kept as their sitting-
room, not that they had much time to use it, but she
felt that they needed a room to call their own. For

her it had been just an ordinary nineteen-hour working day.

It was in March, almost four months later, that the front doorbell sounded one morning and Laurel pulled off her apron and ran upstairs to answer it. The family were all out for once, having set off early that day to spend a long weekend with relations and to attend a family wedding. Even the mother-in-law had been squeezed, endlessly complaining, into the estate car. Laurel had scurried round the house clearing up after them, determined to get through the list of jobs that had been left for her to do before she picked up Troy from nursery school, so that they could enjoy to the utmost this rare holiday. Annoyed at being interrupted, she thought it must be the postman with a parcel; they were always having parcels delivered.

A man stood on the doorstep with his back to her as he sheltered under the shallow porch, his coat collar turned up against the rain. At first she didn't recognise him and said, 'Yes?' expectantly, but then he turned and she found herself looking up into grey eyes underneath blond hair that was wet from the rain. Ross Ashton.

'Hello, Laurel.'

For a few minutes she was too taken aback to speak, wondering how on earth he knew the family she worked for, but then it registered that he had shown no surprise on seeing her. Her silence gave him time to look her over, taking in her frayed jeans and old sweater, the sleeves pushed up to her elbows, her working clothes. Laurel's face paled a little, leaving a flush of embarrassment on her cheeks. Slowly, reluctantly, she said, 'You've come to see me.'

'Yes.'

She shook her head. 'No. I don't care what it is. I don't want to talk to you. I told you to stay away from me.'

'I know. And I've respected your wishes, but something has happened that made me look for you.'

She held up a protesting hand. 'No, I don't want to hear it.'

'I'm sorry, Laurel, but I'm afraid you must.'

For a long moment they stared at each other, Laurel barring his way, her face deathly white, knowing that his being there brought a danger of her life's changing all over again. Ross stood and waited, his eyes on her face, his own features grave. Rain splashed down on to his head, plastering his hair, trickling down his cheek like a tear.

Laurel gave a frightened sob. 'Please go away. *Please*.'

'I can't. It concerns your son.'

'I don't have a son. My brother adopted him. I don't . . .' Her words died away under his gaze and she bit her lip.

'I've been following your trail for months,' Ross told her. 'The first people I tried were your brother and your parents. They said that they had never even seen your child.' He waited and, when she didn't speak, said, 'May I come in?'

Slowly she stepped back into the hall. Ross passed her and closed the door. He looked down at her frightened face and said on a savage note, 'I can't help it if I'm always the bearer of bad news; I don't want to be.'

'What—what bad news?'

But he pulled off his coat and dropped it on a chair, then pushed open the door to the sitting-room. 'Let's go in here.' Taking out a handkerchief, he wiped his face and dried his hair a little, pushing it back from his forehead.

'What is it?' Laurel asked again, all sorts of terrible things going through her mind.

He turned to face her. 'Maybe you already know. Maybe it doesn't matter to you any more. It's Niko. He was killed in a skiing accident last December.'

She stared at him, then turned abruptly away and went to gaze blindly out of the window. Memories of Niko filled her mind: of that day when he had come to meet her at Delphi, young and full of life, and so arrogantly good-looking; with his sleek car, a modern Charioteer. She remembered his almost naked body on the beach, supple and muscular. His laugh, his love of life. All of that, all his shining future, blotted out and gone forever. 'How did it happen?' she asked huskily.

'There was a small avalanche. He and some others were in the way.'

'I see.' Laurel's eyes were wet when she eventually turned to face him, but the tears were for the man she had known, for the tragedy of it, rather than of grief. 'As you said; it does concern my son. Thank you for coming to tell me.'

'Why did you keep the child?' Ross asked curiously.

She smiled. 'The obvious reason; once I saw him I couldn't bear to part with him.'

'From what your parents told me, you had already made up your mind when I saw you in the hospital.'

She nodded. 'As I said; from the first moment I saw him.'

'Why didn't you tell me?' Laurel didn't answer, just looked at him expressively, and Ross sighed. 'You're a very stubborn girl, Laurel. What was so terrible about taking support for your son from his father?'

Her chin came up. 'He rejected me,' she said simply. 'No way was I going to be beholden to a man who didn't love me enough to marry me, who thought I wasn't good enough for him. Or rather, whose father thought I wasn't good enough for him,' she added scornfully. Laurel paused. 'I suppose his father took Niko's death very badly?'

'Yes.' Ross gave her a narrow-eyed look. 'Does that please you?'

Astonishment and distaste filled her face. 'I have a son of my own; I feel terribly sorry for any parent who loses a child. It must be . . .' She shook her head, the appalling tragedy of it too much to comprehend. 'It must be the most dreadful thing that can possibly happen to you.'

Ross turned away from her. They were both still standing, too tense to sit down. 'Niko was Petros's only child. He had pinned all his hopes for the future on him; all the work, all the wheeling and dealing, were for Niko and for the grandchildren he would give him. But Niko was reluctant to settle down; he only got married last year and——'

'Niko was married?' Laurel exclaimed in surprise.

'Didn't you know?' Ross asked, facing her again.

Drily, Laurel said, 'I don't get much time to read the gossip columns.'

'No, I suppose not.' Ross's face tightened. 'As I was saying: Niko and his wife didn't have any children, so Petros Alexiakis has no grandchildren——' he paused deliberately '—except your son. Except Troy.'

It took no more than a second, then, to understand why he had come, and immediate panic swept over her. 'No!' She shouted the word at him, fear filling her face. But then her soul was filled with a black, ungovernable rage. Striding across to Ross, she said, 'You loathsome swine! How dare you come here and ask me to hand over my son after all the trouble you went to to keep him out of Niko's hair? You disgust me.'

The words came out as if she were a snake spitting venom, and Ross's face paled, grew taut. He didn't try to deny why he'd come but said tersely, 'I didn't expect you to say anything else. But Petros won't understand. He thinks that money can buy anything—or anyone.'

'Well, he isn't going to buy my son. He isn't for sale. And if Niko's father tries to bring any pressure on me you can remind him about that precious affidavit he got me to sign. He didn't want to know Troy then and he certainly isn't going to have anything to do with him now.'

'All right, I'll tell him that.'

His mild answer took Laurel by surprise. She was all psyched up to have the biggest fight of her life and Ross had completely thrown her. She glared at him suspiciously. 'And then?'

'And then I'll try to persuade him to accept it.'

'But he won't.'

Ross shook his head. 'No, I'm sure he won't.'

'I'm not going to give up Troy for anyone,' she shot at him, fear and despair in her voice again. 'I'll go away where you'll never find me and——'

'Don't, Laurel. Don't talk like that.' Ross reached out and put a hand on her arm. 'There's no need to run away.'

'Because you'd always be able to find me, I suppose,' she said bitterly.

'Not only because of that. Maybe it will be possible to come to some sort of compromise with Petros.'

'No! I want nothing to do with him. He's—he's a monster.' To Laurel's fevered imagination Petros Alexiakis seemed like a giant black spider with arms that were forever reaching out to harm her.

'Won't you please listen to what he has asked me to say?'

'No, I don't want to hear.' Laurel lifted her hands and put them over her ears, gripping her head. 'Just go away and leave us alone!'

Ross looked at her for a long moment, then gave a curt nod, picked up his coat, and walked out of the room. Quickly Laurel followed him into the hall, still afraid. He put on his coat, said something she didn't hear because she still had her hands over her ears, and then opened the door and left. Laurel rushed to close it behind him, bolting it and putting on the chain for good measure, then leaned against it, her heart beating so loudly that it made her feel faint.

After a few minutes a great sense of loss filled her, but fear for her son soon drove all thoughts of Niko from her mind. Running down to the kitchen, Laurel grabbed up her coat and bag and left the house by the basement entrance. Too impatient to wait for a bus, she took a taxi to the nursery school and rushed inside. The children were sitting on the floor having a story read to them.

'Troy.' She called his name in an agony of fear and nearly collapsed with relief when the child looked round in surprise at her voice. He came to her at once and she caught him to her, her whole body shaking.

'Miss Marland? What is it?' The teacher came over to her, concern in her face.

'Has—has anyone been here asking for Troy?' Laurel stammered.

The woman shook her head, her face clearing; she was used to domestic arguments with children being used as a pawn in the middle. 'No. No one.'

'If a man comes—a tall, blond man. Or any man. Anyone. You won't let them take Troy, will you?'

'Of course not. You should know that.'

Laurel nodded, trembling, and the woman went back to her class, a mixed bag of children of all colours and creeds.

Troy was looking up at her worriedly and somehow she managed to smile at him. 'It's OK, nothing to worry about. Look, as I'm here, why don't you get your mac and we'll go somewhere nice? Where would you like to go?'

'To the toy museum.'

She needn't have asked. He always liked to go to one museum or another. In winter they were the only places they went to, because you didn't have to pay any entrance fee. They got wet walking to the tube station. Looking up at the grey clouds, Laurel wondered when it would ever be spring; the winter seemed to have stretched on endlessly as one long, sodden eternity. This is what hell will be like, she thought, not fire and brimstone, but a rainy day in a London street clogged with cars and buses. But they enjoyed the museum and afterwards, for a treat, went to a McDonald's for a hamburger and chips.

By the time they got back to Hampstead Laurel was feeling more confident. All she had to do was to keep saying no and there was nothing Petros Alexiakis could do about it. By his own hand he had renounced all his family's interests in Troy before he had even been born, and there was no court in the world that would let him take the child away from her now.

That evening they sat in the family sitting-room and watched video films on the television, another rare treat for Troy, but Laurel kept getting up to make sure all the doors and windows were bolted, her feeling of security completely gone.

The next day it actually stopped raining. Laurel was still very nervous and kept going to the windows to look out into the street, but there was no sign of Ross. By lunchtime Troy had become restless, reminding her that she had promised to take him out. Realising that they couldn't stay bolted up like this all the time, Laurel told him to put on his coat, and they went to the zoo. She hadn't slept much the night before, not only because of her fears for Troy, but also because she knew that she ought to tell the child about his father but didn't know how to do it. As soon as he was old enough to understand that other children had fathers he had asked about his own, and Laurel had told him that his father lived in Greece. Troy had been satisfied with that for a while but had recently wanted to know more, and she had explained as best she could without making the boy feel unwanted. He had accepted what she'd said, as children did, but she had known from the look in his dark eyes that there would be more questions when he was older.

Now she put off telling him that Niko was dead; she would tell him after their little holiday, she decided. There was no point in spoiling it for him. But it was spoilt for her when they went to see the lions, which were Troy's favourites, and Ross strolled up to join them. 'Good afternoon, Laurel.' His grey eyes met hers ruefully, then he glanced down at Troy and smiled. 'Hello. You must be Troy.'

The boy nodded, his head arched back as he looked up at Ross's figure towering above him. Ross crouched down to his level, but Laurel took hold of the boy's hand and pulled him away. Troy had been about to smile but looked up at her uncertainly.

'Please don't frighten him off,' Ross said, looking up at her.

But the realisation that he must have followed them there made her voice sharp with anger. 'Go away. Leave us alone.'

Ross straightened up. 'You have a right to be angry, Laurel, but if you'll just hear me out then I'll leave.'

'Huh!' The word was scathing in disbelief.

'You'll frighten the boy,' he pointed out in a half-whisper.

'And you of course are going to take full advantage of the fact,' she said bitingly.

'If I must.'

She looked at him with hate-filled eyes, her glance shrivelling him, but she was trapped and they both knew it.

'Why don't we go and have a coffee?' Ross suggested. 'After you've seen the lions, of course,' he added, glancing down at Troy.

The lions' cages were high off the ground, and Troy constantly wanted to be picked up so that he could see. Laurel did so, although he was heavy for her now and it made her arms ache. Ross wisely didn't offer to help, but it was Troy, annoyed at being set down so quickly, who turned to him and said, '*You* lift me, please.'

Stooping down, Ross put his hands round his waist and lifted him over his head to set him on his shoulders. 'That do?'

Troy laughed delightedly and clutched at his head, but Ross held him firmly by the legs and the boy soon grew confident. After the first stab of fear Laurel looked away, biting her lip, knowing that she mustn't say anything to make Troy afraid, in any sense. When they had seen the lions Troy refused to get down, loving this new aspect of the world, so Ross carried him over to the café and set him down on a chair. 'What would you like?'

Laurel was tempted to grab Troy's hand and run away while Ross was in the queue, but what would be the good? He knew where they lived and could easily follow them there. The knowledge that she was so powerless made her angry again. Coming back with a loaded tray, Ross read it in her eyes, and his mouth twisted sardonically.

He put a glass of milk and a squashy cake in front of Troy, who looked at him with puzzled eyes. 'Are you from Greece?' the boy asked.

Laurel knew immediately what he was getting at, but Ross's eyebrows rose. 'No, I live in London.'

Disappointment filled Troy's eyes and he didn't ask any more questions, just politely thanked him and began to eat.

'Why did he ask that?'

'He knows his father lives in Greece.' She shook her head at his questioning look. 'No, not yet.' For a few moments she concentrated on stirring her coffee, then said coldly, 'You have something to say, haven't you?'

'In a moment. Perhaps Troy would like to have a ride on an elephant after he's finished his cake? He seems to like having rides on tall things,' he added with a grin.

Troy understood and grinned back. He quickly finished his cake and Ross fished in his pocket for some money, but Laurel said sharply, 'I'll pay. Troy isn't allowed to take money from strangers.'

Ross shot her a look from suddenly angry eyes, but allowed her to take out her purse and give some of its rapidly disappearing contents to Troy. 'You can see the queue,' she said. 'Don't push in front. And— and don't leave the queue for anyone. If anyone tries to make you go with them you scream very loudly as I taught you. OK?'

'OK.' He planted an unexpected kiss on her cheek and ran off clutching his money, thrilled by his treat and his independence.

She watched him until he was safely in the queue, then only half turned to Ross so that she could keep an eye on the child while they talked. 'All right, so now carry out your orders, messenger boy,' she said jeeringly.

Ross gritted his teeth. 'One day I'm going to make you apologise for that,' he told her in a flash of anger.

'Why? It's true, isn't it?'

He gave her a smouldering look, his hand balling into a fist, but then he got control again and said shortly, 'Petros Alexiakis wants to make you an offer. He wants you to take Troy to Greece to meet him. Not to Athens but to his island. He understands that you will be reluctant to come, but he assures you that he will make no attempt to take the boy away from you. It will be just for a holiday.'

'And you really expect me to believe that?' Laurel said scornfully. 'He must be mad.'

Ignoring her, Ross went on, 'He admires you for insisting on bringing up the boy alone, but deeply regrets that you wouldn't allow him to help financially. He would like to help you now, for Niko's sake. And——'

'For his own, you mean,' Laurel cut in acidly.

'And he hopes that you will let him pay for Troy to have the standard of education he'll need to run the kind of empire that he might one day inherit.'

'Troy will inherit?' She stared at him in amazement.

'Petros no longer has anyone else to leave it to,' Ross said simply.

For a moment she couldn't take it in, then stood up. 'Tell him to stuff his money,' she said furiously.

A gleam of amusement came into Ross's eyes, but he said gravely, 'Do you have the right to deprive your son of his inheritance?'

'If it means keeping him out of Niko's father's hands, then yes, I do. He didn't know how to bring up his own son and he certainly isn't going to ruin mine! So why don't you run back, like a good little errand boy, and tell him that?' And she turned and strode away, leaving Ross looking after her with the grim look back on his face.

It was Troy's turn for a ride just as Laurel came up to him, so she was able to watch him climb on to the howdah, make sure he was strapped in safely, and then return his excited wave as the patient animal began to lumber along. She didn't look back at Ross, but he had followed her and stood near by, and as Troy waved to him he took out a camera and took a photograph of the boy. It made Laurel even more en-

raged, knowing who the shot was destined for, but
there was nothing she could do about it; unfortunately there was no law against someone taking your
photograph. And at least Ross then raised his hand
to her in a gesture of wry farewell and walked away.
Laurel hoped she had seen the last of him, but with
her kind of luck she very much doubted it.

There was no sign of him, though, the following
day when they went to Hampstead Heath and fed
bread to the ducks, or during the following week when
the family were back home and things were back to
normal again. Laurel began to nurture a faint hope
that maybe Petros Alexiakis had changed his mind,
but she should have known better. On Friday afternoon she was down in the basement beginning the
preparations for a special dinner her employers were
giving for six guests. Troy was sitting on a high stool
at the table, helping her by carefully shelling peas.
His forehead was drawn into a frown of concen-
tration as his little fingers pressed the shells to make
them open and he gave a crow of delighted laughter
every time one made a satisfactory popping noise.

Laurel heard the front doorbell ring, but the mother
was at home and yelled down that she would get it.
But a minute later the woman came into the kitchen
and gave Laurel an odd look. 'There are two men
here to see you. One's called Ross Ashton and the
other has a foreign name I didn't catch.' She saw
Laurel's face go pale. 'Do you know them?' And when
Laurel nodded, 'What do they want? You're not in
any kind of trouble, are you?' she asked sharply.

'No. No, of course not.' Laurel pulled herself
together, her mind racing. So Petros Alexiakis had
come, had he? The great man must be quite deter-

mined if he had taken the trouble to come to England to try to persuade her himself. So Troy must be really important to him. She glanced at her son, carefully taking each pea from its pod. Well, Troy was a darn sight more important to her, and there was no way she was going to let Alexiakis have him.

She became aware that her employer was waiting, and said, 'I'm sorry they came to the front door.'

'They not only came to the front door, they came in a chauffeur-driven Roller,' the woman said, glancing out of the window up to the street. She have Laurel a frankly curious look. 'Who are they?'

But Laurel turned to Troy and told him to go into their sitting-room, not liking the idea of the chauffeur's being able to see him. 'You can put the television on,' she told him. 'But don't come out until I tell you.'

He obeyed her as he always did, especially when one of the family were around; despite his infancy, he knew that there was a gulf between them and the people whose houses they had lived in. When he'd gone, Laurel said, 'I'm sorry. I'll bring them down here.'

'Don't bother, I'll send them down.' The woman gave her an exasperated look. 'But for heaven's sake don't let anything burn while you're talking to them. And keep it brief; you have to go and pick up the children in half an hour.'

'Yes. All right.'

Laurel went over to the oven and took out some hors-d'oeuvres cases she'd been baking, putting them to one side. She was still standing at the oven when she heard footsteps coming down the stairs into the room, one set quick and light, the other heavier.

Laurel gripped hold of the oven rail for a moment, then turned to face, for the first time, Niko's father, Troy's grandfather, the autocrat who had messed up her life.

He was a whole head shorter than Ross, and heavier, too, with thick eyebrows and dark hair turning grey, a swarthy face and full lips. Both men were handsome in different ways, but for an instant Laurel thought she saw some similarity between them, in the jut of the jawline and the strong cheekbones, perhaps. But then the fleeting thought was gone as she recognised much of Niko in his father's features. He was wearing a beautifully cut black overcoat, and carried a black hat. Mourning clothes, Laurel realised. For several long seconds they gazed at each other silently, each weighing the other up, like gladiators waiting to fight. But this was going to be a very unfair contest, because Petros Alexiakis had already lost.

Ross was watching them, and when she glanced at him Laurel was surprised to see amusement in his eyes. She frowned, not understanding, and finding nothing at all funny in the confrontation.

It was Ross who spoke first. 'I don't think I have any need to introduce you. Petros wanted to come and talk to you himself.'

'Really?' Laurel said unhelpfully, tossing her hair back from her face in a gesture that was both proud and defiant.

Petros Alexiakis took a couple of steps further into the room, looking about him, but giving away nothing of his feelings. Most probably he had never been into a kitchen in his life, Laurel thought. So let him slum it for once.

'Miss Marland, I have come myself so that you will know that I am serious in my offer to you.' His English was fluent but he had a strong accent. He was watching her as he spoke and couldn't fail to see the dislike in her eyes. 'You have every reason to hate my family, I know. But my son is dead—and now I wish to do what I can for his son.'

He spread his hands as he spoke, in a gesture inviting sympathy and understanding. But Laurel understood only too well. 'Troy doesn't need anything from you,' she said shortly. 'He never has and he never will. You've already been told that. So please go back to Greece and leave us alone.'

'I'm afraid I can't do that. You see, Niko left a will, and in it he asked me to make provision for his son.'

'Rubbish!' Laurel said at once. 'Because of you Niko wanted nothing to do with him. As far as Niko was concerned Troy had been put out for adoption. Your...' Her eyes rested on Ross's enigmatic features for a moment. 'Your lawyer would have told him that.'

'Nevertheless Niko thought about the child when he made his will,' Petros insisted. 'And I am here to carry out his instructions.' He paused, then, to Laurel's mind, playing for sympathy, said, 'After all, Troy is his only child.'

'And whose fault is that?' Laurel shot back. 'If you hadn't insisted that Niko's other girlfriends had abortions he would probably have had half a dozen children before he died, the way you encouraged him to play around.'

She was pleased to see that Petros was completely disconcerted for a moment by her attack and her openness. He blinked, then shot an angry look at

Ross, who put a hand over the lower half of his face, covering his mouth. Recovering himself, Petros said with an effort, 'Forgive me, Miss Marland, but do you really feel that this place is right for your son? As I understand it you are a servant here, that you have been a servant in other houses. Do you really want to bring up your son to a servant's life?'

'We manage,' Laurel said shortly. 'I do an honest day's work, and I don't take charity, whether it's from you or from the Social Services. I don't see why other people should pay for my mistake.'

'Not even when the father of your son wishes to see that he is properly provided for? That can hardly be called charity.'

'I've already told you: I didn't want anything from Niko and I don't want anything from you,' Laurel said stubbornly, beginning to get angry.

But Petros wasn't to be put off so easily. 'All I am asking is that you come to Greece for a holiday. Get away from this place where it rains all the time for a while, and——'

'No,' Laurel said in annoyance. 'That would be the thin end of the wedge.'

Frowning, Petros switched to Greek and, turning to Ross, said, 'I don't understand what she is saying.'

'It's a colloquialism,' Ross replied in the same language. 'It means that if she gives you an inch you will take a mile.'

He smiled mockingly as he spoke, and Petros gave him a sour look, fully aware of it. 'You were right; she is stubborn,' he commented.

'I said she was proud,' Ross amended.

Laurel understood nearly every word, but was careful not to let them see it. It gave her a feeling of advantage over them. But what surprised her was not only that Ross could speak fluent, unaccented Greek but that he dared to answer his employer so tauntingly.

Petros went to speak again, but just then the door at the top of the stairs opened and her own employer came down a few steps. 'Laurel, it's nearly three o'clock. I'm afraid you'll have to ask your—er—guests to leave so that you can go and pick up the children.'

Laurel obediently began to take off her apron, pleased by the interruption, but Petros said testily, 'We have not yet finished our talk with Miss Marland.'

'Well, I can't help that. I want her to collect my children from school. You'll have to leave.'

At once Petros's shoulders heightened and he spoke with all the force of two thousand years of male chauvinism as he thundered, 'And are you incapable of collecting your own children, woman? Go and get them yourself; I'm not finished here.'

Her employer, who ruled her own husband with a rod of iron wrapped in very worn velvet, gave him a glance of pure astonishment—then meekly turned to obey him!

'Oh, thanks very much,' Laurel said when she'd gone. 'You've most likely cost me my job. I'll have a hell of a time explaining this.'

'So don't explain,' Petros said with sudden fire. 'Why demean yourself? You are as good as her. Better. You don't have to stay here and take her orders. Come to Greece. Let me help you as Niko wanted.'

For a moment Laurel thought he was going to say please. But that would have been begging, and he wasn't the man to do that. And nor was she a woman who could be bought. Her head came up. 'Sorry, no.'

Petros's hands balled into tight fists of exasperation, but after a moment he tried another tack. 'You say that you manage here, Miss Marland, but you used to be a student of archaeology, and quite a brilliant one, so I understand. You were not able to continue with this when Troy was born and you decided to keep him. Would it not be an advantage to both you and your son if you were to finish your studies?'

Laurel flushed, knowing that this was her dearest wish, her secret dream, but valiantly said, 'My son will be deprived of nothing.'

In Greek, Petros said to Ross, 'I think we have found her weakness. Talk to her, persuade her.'

Ross frowned. 'I told you I wanted nothing to do with this.'

'For your own ends,' Petros snapped. The older man suddenly reached out and put his hand on Ross's arm, his grip vice-like. With his build he must have been very strong, but Ross didn't even flinch, just looked coldly into his eyes. Laurel would have frozen under that look, but Petros just shook Ross's arm and said, 'Do as I say,' Adding, his mouth suddenly twisting, 'for Niko's sake.'

For a long moment Ross stared into his face, but then he turned to Laurel and switched to English. 'There is one thing that you're depriving Troy of,' he said slowly. 'You're depriving him of his inheritance.' He held up a hand as she went to object. 'I don't mean the Alexiakis empire. That isn't important. What is important, vital, is that Troy is half Greek and you are keeping his birthright from him. He needs to know Greece. He needs to know his people. You have given him all you can, Laurel; now give him

Greece. Show him his country. Take him to the places where his ancestors lived and fought, built the most glorious civilisation the world has ever known. Can you deny him that, Laurel? Can you? Dare you?'

CHAPTER FOUR

Ross didn't come with the chauffeur-driven car Petros Alexiakis sent to collect them, and Laurel was glad of that. Troy was full of questions and one moment wanted to sit on her lap so that he could see out of the windows, the next wanted to have the safety straps fastened because it made him feel grown up. But over and over again he would ask about the aeroplane. 'Will we soon be at the airport? Is it a jumbo plane? Will I really be able to walk about on it?'

Laurel answered him patiently, her own emotions nearer to dismay than excitement. After the men had gone that day, Laurel had gone up to see her employer who, remembering that she had a dinner party that night, had been prepared to forgive her, so had been even more annoyed when Laurel had given in her notice. 'How ungrateful can you get?' the woman exclaimed. 'After I've taken you in and given you and the boy a home.' If that was home, she could well do without it, Laurel had thought, but didn't bother to say it. That was only two weeks ago; her employer had found someone else and told Laurel to go, that she wanted her rooms for the new housekeeper.

Having foreseen that this might happen, Ross had instructed Laurel to call him at once, but before doing so she had telephoned her parents, wanting to make things up with them, and perhaps in the back of her mind searching, hoping, for an alternative. 'I'm be-

tween jobs,' she told her mother. 'We could come and
stay with you for a few days, if you'd like us to.'

'Really? Well, that would be nice, I suppose,' her
mother answered uncertainly. 'Just a minute; I'll ask
your father.'

She didn't bother to cover the receiver and Laurel
could hear them quite plainly. Her mother seemed
willing for them to come, but her father said, 'And
what do you think Alec and Georgina will say?
They're coming over this Sunday and they won't want
the child flouted in their faces. In between jobs! She
just wants somewhere for her and the boy to live.
Before we know it we'll be saddled with them forever.
And she's had one illegitimate child; what's to stop
her having another? If you want her here, then it's
up to you, but don't blame me if——' Laurel didn't
need to hear any more; she put down the receiver to
save her mother the embarrassment of having to tell
her no.

So where Laurel had thought they would have at
least a month before they went to Greece, here they
were driving in a luxury car to be flown out to Petros's
private island in his private plane. And Laurel was
hating every second of it. At the moment what she
hated most was the display of wealth. She would rather
have been going by bus and tube to the airport and
then joining a queue to check in her luggage like
everyone else. She didn't want Troy to get used to
this, to think that this was how travel ought to be.
The thing that frightened her most was that her young
son would be spoilt by the things that she was sure
Petros would lavish upon him. Spoilt; the word had
little meaning nowadays until you thought about what
it really meant.

Ross was waiting for them at the airport. He came forward to open the door of the car himself and smiled at Troy and said hello. Then he put out a hand to help Laurel, but she ignored it and got out of the car by herself. She had been forced to speak to him over the telephone about the arrangements for this trip, but she had kept the calls to a minimum and her voice brisk and businesslike, letting him know that she spoke to him only on sufferance. He shot her a rather sardonic look, but went round to help the chauffeur unload their luggage. There wasn't much; when you had no roots you didn't acquire much in the way of possessions. Laurel had brought everything that was precious; her photos of Troy when he was a baby, his first drawings, the few books on ancient Greece that she hadn't yet sold, the presents that Niko had given her.

The chauffeur put the luggage on a trolley and Laurel thanked him and said goodbye. It was impossible to be completely aloof, because Troy was so full of excited anticipation of his first flight. And, remembering his ride on his shoulders at the zoo, he treated Ross like an old friend. 'Will I be able to go in the cockpit?' he demanded. 'Mummy says sometimes you can if the pilot says yes.'

'Oh, I'm sure this pilot will say yes,' Ross assured him. 'But not until after we've taken off.'

Troy beamed and wanted to help push the trolley. 'Don't get in the way,' Laurel warned him.

'He isn't in the way,' Ross said shortly. He tried to hold her glance, but she looked quickly away.

Because they were travelling by private plane they walked straight through the concourse to Customs and were then escorted across to where the smaller planes

were parked. The Alexiakis plane wasn't huge by
commercial standards, but it was certainly big enough.
Troy gripped her hand fiercely when he first saw it,
for once overawed, but he returned the smile of the
stewardess who came forward to greet them. Older
than Laurel, the woman gave her a look of bright
curiosity as she took her coat and led her to a seat.
The seats, deeply upholstered in pale blue and very
comfortable, weren't in rows as in a normal aeroplane, but arranged round tables. Despite herself,
Laurel looked round the plane with avid interest; at
the rear of the cabin there was a bar with stools, and
past it, glimpsed through the open door, another cabin
that looked like an office, fitted with telephones, a
computer, a fax machine, and several gadgets she
didn't recognise. Obviously when Petros used the
plane he intended to be fully in touch with all aspects
of his business empire, she thought, trying to be
cynical but not really succeeding.

The stewardess made sure that Troy was securely
fastened into his seat next to Laurel, then went to her
own seat with its back to the cockpit. Laurel looked
round for Ross, but he had gone into the cockpit and
didn't come out. Within a very short time they were
airborne, Troy too excited at seeing the ground falling
away to feel at all frightened.

When they were safely in the air the stewardess came
over. She was heavily made-up, as stewardesses the
world over seemed to be, and her eyes were frankly
assessing, making Laurel aware that her dress was
three years old. 'Can I offer you a drink, Miss
Marland? And perhaps Troy would like something.'

So the stewardess knew who they were; Ross had
told her, Laurel guessed, and had most probably en-

joyed relating his part in persuading her to come. Not that it had been persuasion; it had been pure moral blackmail. Lifting her chin, Laurel said, 'Just coffee, please. And my son will have a glass of orange juice.'

'Of course.' She was soon back with the drinks, a tray of biscuits and little bowls of nibbles. She handed Laurel a menu. 'I'll be serving lunch during the flight. Perhaps you would care to choose what you would like to eat so that I can cook it for you. My name's Tanya, Tanya Crawley. And my husband Mark is the pilot.'

'Will he let me go in the cockpit?' Troy asked anxiously.

Tanya smiled at him. 'I'm sure he will. Especially as Mr Ashton is the co-pilot today.'

She placed a pile of brand new glossy magazines next to Laurel's elbow and some children's books near to Troy and left them alone while they went through the menu. This took some time and a great deal of discussion as each dish had to be described to Troy in detail. Choosing from a menu wasn't something he was used to, and it had been so long for Laurel that she lingered over the choice, savouring the moment but angry with herself for doing so. She must be continually on her guard so that she, too, didn't become 'spoilt'. As she had been during those months with Niko, she realised. Leaning back in her chair, she let her thoughts go back to that time, trying to recall their weeks together. But she had deliberately put him out of her mind for so long that now it was difficult to remember. All that she could picture was Delphi. She longed to go back there one day. And Marathon too. And as she recalled the great plain so Niko came vividly into her mind once more. That had been such a wonderful day, the beginning of their love-affair. Or had it been merely *her* love-affair? Had Niko ever really loved her? Laurel gave a great sigh and put her hand up to cover her face.

'Laurel? Are you all right?' The thick carpeting that dulled the sound of the plane's engines had also deadened the sound of Ross's footsteps, so that she didn't know that he was there until he spoke.

'Yes, of course,' she said shortly, and quickly moved her hand to brush away the hint of a tear, her face a stony mask.

But Ross didn't get the message and go, instead sitting down on the seat opposite hers and leaning forward, his elbows on the table, chin on his hands, to look at her. Disliking his scrutiny, Laurel looked round for Troy and saw that he was in the office with Tanya, being shown all the gadgets. She opened her mouth to call him, wanting him as a safeguard as much as anything, but Ross said brusquely, 'He's all right. Tanya will look after him.' He frowned. 'Are you so unhappy at what you're doing?'

'What I've been coerced into doing, you mean. Yes, of course I'm unhappy. What the hell did you think— that I'd be over the moon at Mr Alexiakis's interest in Troy?'

She spoke angrily, and would have liked to goad him into an argument, but Ross said calmly, 'Petros was telling the truth about Niko's will; he did ask for provision to be made for Troy. I drew it up for him.'

Immediately she wondered if that had been Niko's idea—or his. She remembered that Ross had come to visit her in hospital after she'd had Troy. He had been kind to her then; had he thought that he was still being kind by getting Niko to make provision for his un-

THE GOLDEN GREEK   89

known son in his will? Whichever, they must have
both thought that it would never be necessary; that
Niko would live for a great many years, so it wasn't
any big deal. 'I wish he hadn't,' she said waspishly.
'I wish he'd forgotten all about us.'

'And yet you're here,' Ross reminded her drily.

'Only because of you. Because of your moral
blackmail. Mr Alexiakis would never have thought of
saying what you did about Greece being Troy's
birthright.'

'Probably not,' Ross agreed. 'But he would have
found some other way of luring you to Greece. There's
always a way if someone is determined enough to get
what they want.'

'I don't believe that. It's just an excuse that people
use when they do something immoral. As you did,'
she added scornfully, letting him see her dislike. 'I
shall never forgive you for that. Not that your type
would care, of course.'

Ross's face tightened. 'My type?' he · asked
menacingly.

Laurel should have been warned by that tone but
was too angry to take any notice. 'You're Alexiakis's
yes-man. When he gives an order, you run. And you
don't give a damn what you do or who you hurt in
the process. Why, you even double as a co-pilot.'

Her voice had risen in anger, but Ross reached
across the table and caught her wrist. His grey eyes
were harsh with anger, but his voice was under icy
control as he said, 'Believe it or not, Laurel, making
you unhappy is the last thing I want.'

'I *don't* believe it,' she returned swiftly. 'If you'd
really cared about us you wouldn't have told Alexiakis

where we were. You could easily have told him that you couldn't find us.'

'And then he would have sent someone else to find you. And your trail was easy enough to follow, Laurel. Petros would have caught up with you and things would have worked out just the same. Only he probably wouldn't have used "moral blackmail", as you called it; he would have used outright bribery, and if that didn't work...' Ross shrugged his shoulders expressively, leaving it to her imagination. 'At least you're not here completely against your will.'

What did he mean? Laurel wondered. That Petros would have gone to court to try and get custody of Troy? Or that he would have used threats and intimidation to get them to Greece. Or perhaps just Troy. Laurel was under no illusion that she herself was of any interest to Petros Alexiakis. All he wanted was his grandson, and if she could be bought off or got rid of so much the better. A sudden flash of fear ran through her. She shouldn't have come; she might be walking into some terrible danger.

Ross was still holding her wrist and his grip tightened as he felt her tremble and saw the fear in her eyes. 'I'm sorry, I didn't mean to frighten you. Petros would never knowingly hurt a woman, but he can be—callous. He's very insensitive sometimes, especially when it comes to safeguarding his interests.'

'And you're not, I suppose,' she said bitterly, dragging her arm free.

'You'll fare much better with me to intercede for you than you would alone.'

Laurel gave a heavy sigh and pushed her hair back from her face. She felt a great weight of loneliness and would have liked to believe him; she certainly needed a friend. 'Will you really help me?'

'All I can,' Ross assured her, his face lightening.

Looking at his hard, strong features, Laurel suddenly wanted to believe him. It would be good to have him on her side. But she was far from trusting him. She sighed again and said, 'I shouldn't have come. I should have moved on somewhere where you couldn't find us.'

'But I would have—eventually. Petros would never have given up.'

'And you would have told him again, I suppose.'

'I would have had to.'

He was watching her steadily, his grey eyes waiting for her reaction. Laurel frowned. 'Why, if you're really concerned about us?'

Ross gave a short mirthless laugh, the accompanying shrug as expressive as that of a Greek. 'Because I'm closer to him than I am to you.'

She stared at him, then said in a tone of utter derision, 'So much for your offer of protection! Why don't you go back and help fly the plane? You are the *hired help* after all.'

The words sounded as insulting as they were meant to. Getting to his feet, Ross said curtly, 'I came to see if Troy would like to go in the cockpit now.'

He went to get the boy, leaving Laurel to open one of the magazines and gaze down at it unseeingly. She wasn't proud of that last gibe; after all, she had been nothing more than a hired help herself for more than four years. Perhaps Petros had been good to Ross. And there was nothing wrong with loyalty to one's employer, even if the employer was as ruthless and domineering as Petros Alexiakis. But it didn't make

her feel any less antagonistic towards Ross. She tried
not to think about him, but couldn't help being
puzzled; he was obviously clever if he was a qualified
lawyer, and it was unusual that he spoke fluent Greek.
But perhaps that was why he'd been picked to represent the Alexiakis interests. What mostly baffled her
about Ross was his attitude towards Petros; it certainly wasn't that of a subservient employee. There
had been mockery in his tone more than once when
he'd spoken to him, and, when they'd been speaking
Greek, open antagonism that was little short of defiance. Surely no employer, especially one as rich as
Petros, would have tolerated such an attitude from
an underling, even one as useful and loyal as Ross
evidently was? And how could he possibly be loyal
and defiant all at the same time?

The puzzle was too much for Laurel to think about
when she had so many other worries on her mind;
she pushed it aside and joined in Troy's excitement
when he came back from his visit to the cockpit. He
had actually been allowed to fly the plane, he told
her. 'I sat on Ross's lap and turned the wheel.'

'You did? How marvellous. But I really think you
ought to call him Mr Ashton, don't you?'

'No, because I've given him permission to call me
Ross,' the owner of the name informed her as he came
to sit with them.

It was time for lunch and he obviously intended to
join them. Troy demanded his attention, talking about
the plane, as Tanya served them. Ross answered all
his questions as if Troy were fourteen instead of four,
only explaining more simply if Troy frowned in in-
comprehension. After they'd eaten Tanya showed
Laurel a bathroom and sleeping cabin, both as

luxuriously appointed as the main cabin. After they
had thoroughly explored, Laurel tucked Troy up for
a nap. She kissed him, then hesitated before saying,
'Darling, I want you to do something for me. When
we get to Greece I want you to pretend that we don't
speak any Greek at all. Will you do that for me?'

Troy nodded, not understanding. 'Is it a game?'

'A sort of game, yes. Maybe one day, when we
know Mr Alexiakis better, we'll surprise him. But not
yet. OK?'

'OK.' He grinned and lay back on the pillow willingly enough. He had been too excited to sleep much
the night before and he soon fell asleep as she read
him a story.

Leaving him, she went back into the cabin,
expecting Ross to have returned to the cockpit, but
he was using the phone in the office. Seeing her, he
put the phone down and came to join her.

'Reporting back to Alexiakis, I suppose?' she said
acidly.

'No, I was calling my mother, as a matter of fact.'

His reply made her feel foolish. 'Oh. I didn't realise
you had a mother.'

Ross's lips twitched in amusement. 'Most people
do.'

She wanted to laugh with him, but instead turned
away and said, 'When does the pilot get to eat?'

'Now, I think.'

Her eyes widened, 'While he's flying?'

'The plane is on automatic pilot. It's quite safe.'

'Oh, yes, of course.'

'Perhaps you'd like to know something about the
island where you'll be staying, and the people you're
likely to meet,' Ross offered.

But she wasn't ready to meet him even halfway and said shortly, 'No, thanks. I'm really not interested.' Crossing to a chair, she sat down, picked up another magazine and held it in front of her, rudely shutting him out.

'As you like.' Ross turned and went back to the cockpit.

They didn't see him again until after the plane had landed at Naxos. The airport was small and they had to walk across the tarmac. 'It's hot!' Troy exclaimed in surprise. Compared to England, it was, of course, but for Greece it was a mild spring day.

Taking his hand, Laurel smiled down at him. 'Welcome to Greece.'

They were escorted through Customs and passport control as if they didn't exist, Ross walking beside them and just using the phrase 'Guests of Mr Alexiakis' to make everyone jump to help them. It was difficult not to be impressed, but Laurel did her best and largely succeeded. Another chauffeur-driven limousine—it was so long you could hardly call it a car—was waiting for them outside the airport. Ross waited for her to get in ahead of him but Laurel hung back. 'What about our luggage?'

'It will follow on,' Ross assured her, and gestured towards an estate car parked behind the limo.

They all got into the back of the car, but there was so much room it was like a caravan.

'Where are we going now?' Troy demanded.

'Now we take a boat ride to Temenos, where Mr Alexiakis lives. And yes, you will be allowed to steer it,' he added as Troy opened his mouth to ask.

The boy laughed and turned to Laurel to share his amusement so that she had to smile back.

'That didn't hurt too much, did it?' Ross remarked. She didn't pretend not to understand, but
turned to look fixedly out of the window. Ross observed her for a few moments, then said, 'A word of
warning, Laurel. Petros likes women to appear happy
even if they're not. You'll get on much better with
him if you relax this "holier-than-thou" attitude and
meet him halfway.'

'I should have thought that coming all the way to
Greece was a lot more than meeting him halfway,'
Laurel flashed back.

'You know what I mean. And I would advise you
not to use the boy as a pawn.'

Laurel gave a short laugh. 'Isn't it strange how
people always insist on giving advice even when they
know that no one is going to listen?'

A grim look came into Ross's eyes, and he didn't
speak to her again, talking to Troy instead, until they
reached the harbour where all the boats were moored.
Most of them were fishing boats, the local caique
prominent among them. But there was one that stood
out, a big motor cruiser with a flying bridge, sleek,
powerful and beautiful. Without being told, Laurel
knew that the boat must be the one they were heading
for. It was called the *Irini*. Named after Petros's wife,
she guessed. Funny, she hadn't given a thought to
Troy's grandmother before. Couldn't even remember
Niko speaking about his mother. It had always been
his father, what his father would say, what he would
think.

Troy's eyes were popping, taking everything in, but
he responded to the greeting of the captain, who was
waiting on deck to meet them, with a polite, 'Good
afternoon,' and a handshake. Laurel got her hand

shaken too, and a big grin from the hefty-looking Greek. But she was surprised to see that Ross got not only an enthusiastic handshake but also a comradely hug of welcome and a torrent of Greek.

They discarded their coats and Ross took them all round the boat, but Laurel liked it best on deck where the breeze lifted her hair. She stayed there, holding the rail, watching Naxos gradually disappear from sight, while Ross took Troy up to the bridge. I'm in Greece again, she thought. I'm really here at last. But the pleasure the thought brought her was swiftly outweighed by a dread of what was to come. Again she felt very alone and vulnerable. I mustn't let Petros intimidate me, she thought. I have to stand up to him for Troy's sake. But maybe it would be better not to show outright antagonism. After all, he was Troy's grandfather, and for the boy's sake it would be wiser not to create an atmosphere of tension all the time. Without consciously doing so, Laurel heeded Ross's advice, and when the boat docked at Temenos she was prepared to meet Petros, if not halfway, then at least without open defiance.

Laurel wasn't at all sure what she expected a private island to be like. Based on watching films and television, her thoughts were that it would probably be a small island, with just one house, and well protected against casual visitors. So she had a surprise when, only half an hour or so later, the boat sailed into a horseshoe-shaped harbour with a jumble of houses climbing the steep face of the surrounding hillside. Simple cubes painted white or blue, the houses clung to the cliffs, looking in imminent danger of sliding down to the broad pavement that edged the waterfront. As they came nearer Laurel saw that there were shops and tavernas stretching around the harbour, and she glimpsed little cobbled lanes running between the houses from the waterfront up the hill. Halfway up, there were the white domes of two churches that faced each other across the width of the town, like two mother hens gathering their children around them. Here and there an olive tree provided shade, but mostly the little port lay open to the sun and the sea. A very simple town, and very beautiful.

When the boat was moored and they prepared to disembark, Laurel couldn't help saying to Ross, 'It's so different to what I expected. I didn't think there could possibly be a town on a private island.'

'Just because Petros owns it doesn't mean that he was going to stop the natives of the island living here,' Ross answered.

'I just didn't think there would be any other people.'

'It's been settled for over three thousand years. There's quite an interesting archeological site over the other side of the island where there used to be an old harbour before an earthquake destroyed it. And I think this harbour has been in use for well over a thousand years.' He gave her a brief glance. 'Petros is too much of a Greek to interfere with that.'

Another car was waiting for them on the quay, but a far more practical estate car this time. They were driven through the town and up the widest of the cobbled streets, winding its way between the houses where black-clad women standing at doors and windows and men sitting outside tavernas looked up curiously as they passed. The sound of the car's engine reverberated from the walls as the driver changed gear to climb the steepest part of the slope, and then they had reached the top and had a breathtaking view of the sea as the road ran parallel with the cliff top for about a mile. Then it turned inland for a short way and entered an area where trees and flowering shrubs had been planted in lavish profusion. They drove through this garden for quite a way before the road turned and they arrived at the most beautiful Mediterranean villa Laurel had ever seen.

It was white, of course, and only two storeys high, roofed with faded red pantiles, and the doors and shutters were of varnished wood, with ornate iron grilles at the windows. That was to put it at its simplest. But it was also very large and sumptuous, having the aura of richness that only money and constant care could give. But for all its grandness it had mellowed to fit in perfectly with the garden and the landscape.

When Troy saw it his hand stole into Laurel's and she looked away from the house to give him a hug and an encouraging smile.

She had expected Petros to be there waiting for them, eager to see his grandson for the first time, but there was only a housekeeper in a smart navy blue dress waiting on the steps.

'This is Thespina,' Ross introduced her. The housekeeper smiled at him, and Ross bent to kiss her on both cheeks, affection in his eyes. 'She will take good care of you and see that you have everything you want.'

'If you will come this way, *kyria*.'

Still holding Troy's hand, she was led into the house, Laurel expecting to be confronted by Petros at any moment, but instead they were taken to a suite of two bedrooms with a bathroom in between, and, off the main bedroom, a dressing-room that was lined with fitted wardrobes, each faced with a full-length mirror. Laurel gulped at the sheer luxuriousness of it all and held Troy's hand for her own reassurance now.

'I expect you would like to bathe and change,' Thespina said in good English. 'Your cases should be here at any moment. Ah, yes.' There was a knock on the door and she went to open it. The chauffeur carried in their shabby cases, one of them held together with a leather belt, and put them on the floor. 'I will unpack for you.'

'Oh, no, please.' Laurel quickly held out her hand to stop her. 'I'll do that.'

'As you please,' Thespina replied tranquilly. 'If you will ring when you're ready I will show you over the rest of the house.'

'Thank you.'

As soon as the door had shut behind her they both turned and ran to the bathroom. 'What is it? Is it a paddling-pool?' Troy demanded, gazing enthralled at the huge circular marble bath set on a dais of cream carpeting and bright with gold taps and fittings.

'No, I think it's a jacuzzi. You get lots of bubbles. Like this.' Laurel turned the taps experimentally while Troy crowed with excitement. 'Yes, that's it. Look.' The water began to froth very satisfactorily. Laurel saw a big bottle of bath foam and poured some in, making the water bubble into layers of candy-floss. They both gave a cry of delight and Laurel said, 'Quick, take your things off and jump in.'

'You too. You too.'

There was plenty of room for both of them and they romped and played until Laurel felt guilty about the way they were soaking the carpet and called a halt. They dressed quickly then, putting on the best clothes they had, and Laurel went to put their things away in the cupboards and drawers, but was surprised to find that there were a lot of women's clothes already stored there. Maybe this room was usually used by a member of Petros's family. Whoever she was she had good taste, and expensive taste too, of course; all the clothes bore designer labels and were still in their plastic wrappers so looked like new. Conscious of the length of time they'd spent in the bath, Laurel managed to restrain her natural feminine curiosity and gave the clothes only a cursory look before finding an empty cupboard in which to put her own things. They all looked even drabber now.

Collecting Troy, who was twiddling with the television set, she rang the bell, and Thespina came after only a couple of minutes. She smiled at them, a calm, placid smile of someone who was perfectly content. She led them through the house, telling them about its history. They saw the courtyard with its outdoor pool set amid trellises of trailing bougainvillaea, the full-size indoor pool and the gymnasium opening off it. The billiard-room, the breakfast-room, opening on to a terrace that had the most magnificent view out over the sea, the sitting-room, the dining-room, and finally the drawing-room where Ross was sitting, reading through some papers.

Putting the papers back in his briefcase, he got to his feet as soon as they came in, and smiled when he noticed their still damp hair. He, too, had changed and was wearing a pair of light-coloured trousers, a shirt open at the neck and with the sleeves rolled up, and a pair of trainers. Discarding his usual business suit somehow made him seem more human, more approachable. 'How about a drink on the terrace?' he suggested.

The afternoon sun shone directly on to the terrace and there was still a great deal of warmth in it even though it was well into the afternoon. Ross served the drinks himself from a bar in the drawing-room, then came out to sit beside her, while Troy wandered around, exploring, but coming frequently back to make sure that she was safely waiting for him.

'I'm sorry Petros wasn't here to meet you,' Ross told her. 'Unfortunately he's been delayed, but he hopes to be here in time to join you for dinner.'

It wasn't a prospect that Laurel looked forward to, but at least he wasn't here yet. 'This is a beautiful place,' she said dreamily, lifting her face to the sun.

'I hoped you'd like it.'

She sat for a few minutes with her eyes closed, then turned to Ross. 'Would you do something for me?'

A rueful look came into his eyes. 'If I can.'

'You mean if it doesn't interfere with Mr Alexiakis's interests,' Laurel said wryly.

'I'm afraid so, yes.'

She gave a twisted little smile. 'Oh, I don't think what I want will strain *your* self-interest.' His eyes darkened and she sighed. 'Sorry, I suppose I shouldn't have said that.'

His eyebrows rose. 'An apology? I can hardly credit it. But as you obviously meant what you said it was hardly worth the bother of apologising, was it?'

Laurel turned to fully look into his face. His features seldom showed any emotion, always held under stern control, but it was his eyes and his voice that sometimes gave him away. There were deep feelings there, hidden, but definitely there. And there was a steely strength underlying his cool composure that she envied. 'I wish . . .' she said slowly, but then broke off, not sure herself what it was she wished.

Ross waited for her to go on and, when she didn't, said, 'You asked me to do something for you.'

'Oh, yes.' She frowned and looked down at the table, her finger drawing an abstract pattern on its surface. 'After you came to find me and told me about Niko's death, I went to a library and looked up the back numbers of the papers; found out all I could about what had happened. There wasn't much, but one paper did say that his body was brought here to be buried.'

Ross's eyes shadowed for a moment before he nodded. 'Yes.' Getting to his feet, he took her arm and led her along the terrace that went along the whole side of the house that faced the sea. Taking her to the left-hand end where they could also see inland, he pointed across the gardens to where she could just see the top of a white-domed chapel, similar to those in the town. 'That's the family chapel,' Ross said brusquely. 'Beside it there's a small graveyard. That's where they brought him home to.'

'Would you take us there?'

'Us?' he asked with a frown.

'Yes.' Laurel hesitated, then decided to confide in him and said, 'I think it's about time that I told Troy about his father.'

A warm look came into Ross's eyes. 'Yes,' he agreed. 'I certainly think you should.'

The three of them walked together through the gardens, Troy in the middle, somehow aware of the solemnity of the occasion, and walking quietly, his hand in Laurel's. But when they had only walked twenty yards or so, he reached up and put his free hand in Ross's, looking up at him for reassurance. Ross smiled down at him, a suddenly vivid smile that made Laurel's eyes widen and gave her a strange feeling that was completely new to her and she couldn't describe.

The chapel doors were standing open and Ross led them inside. It was very cool, the fittings very simple. Candles burned under a beautifully painted icon and a shaft of sunlight fell from the window on to the altar. They paused for a moment, looking round, then Ross led them through another door into the small high-walled graveyard. He pointed to a stone set in the shade of an overhanging tree, agonisingly new among the other, weathered stones. 'There,' he said. 'Under the tree of heaven.'

She went forward alone at first, and stood looking down at the inscription on the plain white stone. It was in Greek, of course, and for a few moments Laurel found that her eyes were blurred with tears and she couldn't read it. She blinked hard and read an inscription as simple as the stone: 'Nikolaos Alexiakis', and the years of his birth and death. So few years. Half turning, she held out her hand to Troy, and as he came to her Ross turned and left them alone.

Squatting down to his level, Laurel said, 'You remember I told you your father came from Greece?' The boy nodded and his eyes suddenly widened as he looked towards where Ross had been standing. 'No, you know what your father looked like; I showed you his photograph. And you know his name wasn't Ross, it was Niko.'

'Is he here? Am I going to see him?' Troy's body was suddenly tense.

'No, darling. I'm afraid you're never going to see him now. You see, he was in a terrible accident and he died. This is where he's buried,' and she indicated the grave.

His small body came close to hers and he put his arm round her neck, digging his fingers into her skin.

'It's all right,' she told him firmly. 'It's very sad that he's dead, but he's happy now that he's back here on this lovely island. Because this is where he lived when he was a little boy like you. He played here in the garden and swam in the pools. He loved it here, he often told me so, and he's happy that he's going to stay here forever.'

'Tell me about him again,' Troy demanded.

It was a story that she had told him often; about how she and Niko had met in the ancient ruins and had fallen in love, but Niko had had to go away before he was born and couldn't come back. A very romanticised version of the truth, but enough to make Troy proud of his parentage instead of hiding it away like something small and shameful.

She was still telling him the story when she heard footsteps behind them and turned, expecting to see Ross. But it was Petros Alexiakis, dressed in a dark business suit, his black tie proclaiming his continued mourning, his face set into hard, expectant lines.

Standing, Laurel put her hands on Troy's shoulders and said, 'Darling, this is Mr Alexiakis. He is Niko's father. Your grandfather.'

CHAPTER FIVE

LAUREL was very proud of Troy; he could easily have flinched away or become babyish, but he looked up at Petros with a brave if uncertain stare. The man gazed down at him for a long moment without showing any reaction, but then the hard mask of his face crumpled and his mouth worked as if he was striving to control his emotions. His voice harsh, Petros finally said, 'You are very like your father.' Then he went down on one knee, putting a hand up to the corners of his eyes and swiftly away again as he did so. 'Will you give your old grandfather a kiss?' he demanded, opening his arms.

Troy pressed back against Laurel's legs; he wasn't used to men and had never kissed anyone except Laurel in his life. For a moment she thought he was going to refuse, but then he laughed and stepped forward to put his arms round Petros's neck. Petros gave a great shout and stood up, hugging Troy fiercely. Laurel saw tears come into his eyes again and quickly walked away, leaving them to get to know each other, and knowing instinctively that Petros wouldn't want anyone to see his vulnerability at this moment.

She walked back through the gardens and came to a fountain and an arbour set under a great trail of flame-coloured bougainvillaea. Ross was sitting there, apparently just lazing in the last of the sun, but she knew he was waiting for her. He raised an eyebrow when he saw she was alone. 'That was very courageous of you.'

'What was?'

'To leave Troy alone with Petros.'

'I would have been an intruder,' Laurel said shortly. But nevertheless she glanced back towards the chapel, afraid that Troy might need her, half hoping that he did.

Leaning forward, Ross took hold of her hand and drew her to the seat beside him. 'Petros won't harm him.'

'Troy isn't used to men. He might be frightened.'

'Then Petros will put him at his ease,' Ross said calmly. 'The Greeks love children; you should know that.'

Laurel gave a sarcastic laugh. 'Not from *my* experience, they don't. And especially Mr Alexiakis.'

Ross looked rueful. 'Ah, yes.' But then he grinned. 'But your determination not to have an abortion beat Petros then and I have every confidence in your doing so now.'

'Is this a contest, then?' Laurel asked sharply . 'A fight for my son?'

Ross laughed. 'The second battle of Troy!'

'It isn't funny!' Laurel snapped.

His smile faded and Ross gave her an assessing look. 'You knew what you were up against when you came here, Laurel. Petros will try and keep Troy in Greece, with or without you. But he has absolutely no legal rights, so you can take the boy away whenever you want. And that, of course, is your second weapon. Whenever Petros tries to coerce you, just threaten to leave.'

'You said "my second weapon"; what, then, is my first?'

'The love you have for the boy and he for you. It shines out of you both.' His eyebrows flickered. 'And I pity any man who tries to come between you, whether it's Petros wanting Troy—or a lover wanting you.'

Laurel raised surprised eyes at that, but Ross's face was completely enigmatic. I wish I could tell what he's thinking, Laurel thought in sudden frustration. I wish I could see past that cool mask he always wears.

As if he could read her thoughts, Ross gave a small smile and picked up her hand. 'Oh, by the way: welcome back to Greece.' And he bent to her hand, turning it over so that he kissed her palm, his eyes holding hers as he did so.

A flush started to creep up her cheeks, but the next second Ross let go her hand and stood up. Speaking in Greek, he said, 'So, Petros, you have found your grandson.'

Laurel turned, only now aware that they weren't alone. Petros had Troy by the hand, but when she smiled and held out her arms the boy let go and ran to her. 'He cried a lot,' he whispered in her ear.

'That's because he's so pleased to see you.'

'And he said some Greek. He said, "My son lives again," but I didn't tell him that I could understand.'

'Good for you.' She gave him a hug and smiled at him.

'Miss Marland.' Petros came up and nodded to her. 'I must thank you for bringing Troy here.'

'We're *both* pleased to be here,' she returned, emphasising that Troy wasn't alone.

His dark eyes met her challenging green ones and he nodded in understanding. A faint glint of amusement, the first Laurel had seen him show, came into his face and he said, 'You are *both* very welcome to Temenos.'

'Perhaps we should go back to the house now,' Ross said into the little silence that followed. 'I should imagine Troy is getting hungry.' Stooping down, he put his hands round Troy's waist and swung him high into the air, then set him on his shoulders, the boy giving a shriek of delight.

Petros gave an exclamation of annoyance, but Ross merely looked at him with a grin of mockery. His eyes flicked to Laurel for a moment and then he turned and strode ahead of them through the garden, holding Troy's hand and bouncing him on his shoulders, much to the boy's enjoyment. Nothing had been said, but with that one small gesture Laurel felt a sudden glow of warmth; it was as if Ross had openly said, Look, I'm on your side. She could almost have felt sorry for Petros at that moment, but one look at the angry menace in his eyes and she soon changed her mind.

They followed on more slowly and Laurel said diffidently, 'Your island is very beautiful, Mr Alexiakis. Just as I expected it to be.' He didn't speak and she said, 'Niko often told me about it.'

That, too, was a challenge.

Petros turned his head to look at her, his hair naturally curly, his skin deeply lined and tanned dark from the sun. 'I'm glad you went to see my son's grave.'

'I had to tell Troy that his father was dead. And I—I wanted to say goodbye.'

She didn't look at him as she spoke; she didn't want to see the derision that might be in his eyes. Increasing her stride, she caught up with Ross and Troy, who was reaching up to break off a flower from a tree, which he solemnly presented to her.

'Thank you, kind sir.' And she dropped him a curtsy, making the boy give a crow of laughter.

When they reached the villa Thespina was waiting to show them to a small room at the back of the house where Troy was to have his meal. 'I'll stay with him, if you like,' she offered.

Laurel smiled but said, 'Thanks; perhaps another day.'

Troy's head started to droop almost before he'd finished eating, so Laurel picked him up and carried him to his bedroom, skipping another bath and letting him go straight to bed. She stayed with him for a few minutes until he was deeply asleep, looking down at his young, innocent face, wondering yet again whether she had done the right thing in bringing him here.

Thespina had said that dinner was at eight-thirty. With time to spare, Laurel had another look at the clothes in the wardrobe, even more intrigued to know who they belonged to. Whoever the woman was, she took the same size as Laurel. Niko had no sisters, of course, and she couldn't remember him ever talking about any cousins. Then it hit her. They must have belonged to Niko's wife! She'd almost forgotten that he'd been recently married before he was killed, hadn't given that other woman in Niko's life a thought. Laurel wondered why she hadn't been buried beside Niko. Perhaps her parents had wanted her to be buried in their own family plot, especially as the marriage had been such a short one. A sudden shiver ran down her spine and Laurel quickly closed the wardrobe door; she didn't much like the idea of the clothes being there now.

Turning away, it occurred to her that these rooms might have been the rooms that Niko and his wife had used before their deaths. That, too, sent a shiver of revulsion down her spine. If so, whoever had decided to give them these rooms must be very insensitive. How could anyone put Niko's ex-mistress and her child in a room where Niko had brought his bride, let her sleep in the bed that had been his bridal bed? Could it have been Petros that had ordered it? But surely not, surely he wasn't that hard, that—cruel? Laurel froze, suddenly afraid that this might be a deliberate ploy to embarrass her, to make her feel unsettled and uncomfortable in the one place where she would have sought peace.

No, it couldn't possibly be like that. She was jumping to stupid conclusions because she was tired and nervous. Annoyed with herself, Laurel tried to shake off the mood. She brushed the long swathe of her tawny hair, and fastened it back off her face, repaired her make-up, and stood back to look at herself in one of the long mirrors. The dress would have to do. It wasn't bad; she'd bought it in a nearly new shop a couple of years ago and its leaf-green colour complemented her eyes. She thought again of the clothes in the wardrobe and the huge gulf between Niko's mistress and his bride. But at least she was alive!

After checking on Troy, Laurel found her way back to the main sitting-room. Now that the sun had gone down there was a chill in the air, but the villa had central heating, the curtains were drawn against the night and there was a fire burning in the large stone fireplace. Laurel walked towards it and only then noticed that Ross was sitting in one of the big arm-chairs, its back towards the door. She gave him a brief smile and said, 'I haven't seen an open fire for years. They seem to be a luxury for only the rich nowadays.'

'Or the very poor,' Ross remarked.

She nodded and held out her hands to the blaze.

'Is Troy OK?'

'Yes. Fast asleep. It's all been rather too much for one day.'

'Would you like a drink?'

Laurel shook her head and gave him a curious look; he seemed to make himself completely at home in this house where he was only an employee, not even a guest. He had changed for dinner and was wearing a white tuxedo that fitted him perfectly and made him look—Laurel sought for a word and came up with affluent. As if he was as rich and as much part of the jet set as Petros. 'You said that you'd known Niko all his life,' she said slowly, trying to work it out in her mind. 'But surely you can't have been working for Mr Alexiakis for that length of time? You can't be old enough.'

'Hardly.' Ross's lips curled with amusement. 'No, you could say that I'm—connected with the family.'

'Oh. I see.' But Laurel didn't, of course. She waited, but it seemed that Ross wasn't about to explain further, so she didn't feel that she could ask. Changing tactics, she said, 'You once offered to tell me about the people I was likely to meet here.'

'And you said that you weren't interested.' Ross gave her a mocking look over the top of his glass as he took a drink. 'Changed your mind?'

'Reluctantly.' She gave a small shrug. 'Anyway, there seems to be only Mr Alexiakis here that I need to know about. Unless Niko's mother is here too. Although Niko never mentioned his mother to me.'

'No, she left Petros for good about ten years ago.'

'For good?'

'Yes, she'd left and he'd brought her back a couple of times before she managed to make a final break. He wouldn't divorce her, though, so neither of them could marry again. Perhaps it suited them both that way. It certainly suited Petros.'

'You mean it gave him a clear field without the danger of getting caught,' Laurel said drily.

Ross's eyes settled on her for a moment. 'Such cynicism in one so young. But yes, you're right. He did play the field for a few years. As for Niko's mother, her name is never mentioned. She lived in America until she died a couple of years ago.'

'So there's no one here except you and Mr Alexiakis?'

'There is one other.' Ross gave her a speculative look. 'I wasn't sure if she was here or not, but it seems that she came over from Athens specially to meet you.'

'She?'

'Yes.' Ross was about to go on but he heard the door open behind him and looked round, then stood up. 'And here she is.'

A young woman walked into the room, obviously Greek from her dark colouring, about the same age as Laurel and wearing a beautiful black velvet dress. Her hair was drawn back from her head in a very sophisticated style, and she wore round her neck, the stones brilliant against the black velvet, the most amazing river of diamonds and rubies that Laurel had seen outside of the crown jewels. Matching bracelets on each wrist caught the light as the girl walked in, immediately followed by Petros. There was a haughty almost disdainful look on her face, but avid curiosity in the eyes that swept over Laurel.

Walking forward, Petros said to her, 'This is Miss Marland.'

And Ross said, 'Laurel, this is Irini, Niko's widow.'

'Madame Alexiakis,' the girl snapped.

Laurel looked at her in amazement, then turned to Ross. 'But I thought Niko's wife must have died with him.' He shook his head and Laurel's voice hardened. 'It didn't occur to you to just mention that she was here, I suppose?'

Leaning forward, Ross said softly, so that only she could hear, 'But you weren't interested. Remember?'

She shot him a furious look and then turned back to the other girl. 'How do you do?' she said stiltedly.

Irini merely gave the briefest of nods and crossed to sit on the sofa. 'A Bacardi, Stavros.'

Laurel looked round, expecting to see a servant, but it was Ross who said in some amusement, 'Petros, your daughter-in-law would like a drink.'

A second pair of eyes, dark ones this time, flashed at Ross in anger. Laurel felt completely bewildered. Why had Irini called him Stavros? And how could Ross possibly refuse to obey her? She looked at Irini again and realised that she must surely be overdressed for a family dinner in a holiday villa. So were the velvet dress, the diamonds, and the sophisticated hairstyle all meant to emphasise the gap between them? Were they meant to put her, Laurel, firmly in her place as the lowest of the low? Anger and resentment tightened her features as she looked at Ross

again, but he returned her gaze steadily and she suddenly remembered what he'd said about her having
two weapons, and a wave of pity for the other girl
ran through her. Niko was dead and would never give
Irini a child, but Laurel had Troy, with everything
that meant for a woman. She became aware that Ross
was still watching, waiting, and she gave a small sigh,
her shoulders relaxing.

He gave a nod of approval. 'Perhaps you'd like a
drink now?'

'Yes, please.' She lifted her chin. 'A gin and tonic,
please.'

'I'll get it.' Petros spoke from the bar.

Irini had been watching the interchange of glances
and Laurel had the strange idea that she didn't like
what she'd seen, but she said politely enough, 'You
had a pleasant journey here, Miss Marland?' Irini's
eyes went over her assessingly as she spoke, the
scrutiny so minute that Laurel was sure the Greek girl
had spotted the slight tear in the skirt of the green
dress that she'd so carefully tried to mend.

'Very pleasant, thank you.' Laurel actually wondered for a moment if she ought to offer condolences
on Niko's death. Lord, what a situation! Petros came
over with the drinks and then stood by the other armchair, on the other side of the fireplace next to Ross's,
obviously waiting for Laurel to sit down. The only
place was next to Irini on the settee.

'Your son is a very sweet little boy,' the other girl
remarked.

'You've seen him?' Laurel asked in surprise.

'Yes. I saw him asleep in his bed just now.' And
Irini gave her a look of malicious enjoyment.

Rage filled Laurel's heart and it would have been easy to be rude, but there were better ways than that. All compassion disappeared completely as she made her voice honey-sweet and said, 'He's very like his father, isn't he? Ross said that he's exactly like Niko was at that age.'

Anger shone in Irini's eyes. She put a hand up to her throat, felt the necklace, and her face changed. 'This is one of the pieces of jewellery that Niko gave me for a wedding present,' she remarked. 'He was so generous, always showering me with presents.'

'Yes,' Laurel agreed. 'He was always giving me things, too.'

Irini's eyebrows rose. 'Jewellery?'

'Oh, no. Things that *really* mattered, things that meant something to us both.'

Their polite slanging-match might have got out of hand then, but luckily Thespina came in to announce that dinner was ready. Petros went to Irini's side to escort her in and Ross came to take Laurel's glass from her. 'A clash of the Titans,' he said in amusement.

She gave him a withering look. 'I suppose you think it's all very funny. Why didn't you warn me that she'd be here?'

'I didn't know myself until we arrived. Petros doesn't always tell me about these little surprises he cooks up.'

'Look, there are things I don't understand.'

He put his hand on her arm. 'After dinner,' he said soothingly.

The meal was a constrained one, with Ross thankfully doing most of the talking, telling Laurel about the history of the island. He seemed to know an awful

lot. 'You must take Laurel and Troy to see the ancient
site,' he said to Petros. 'As a Greek classicist, Laurel
will be very interested.'

'Of course. We will go tomorrow, if you wish,'
Petros answered.

Irini raised her brows. 'You are a classical scholar?
You have a degree?'

'Unfortunately, no.' Laurel shook her head. 'Troy
was born just before I was due to take my exams, so
I never did get my degree.'

'How convenient,' Irini commiserated, then gave a
little laugh and put her hand to her mouth. 'Oh, but
my English is wrong; I meant inconvenient, of course.'

Laurel gave her a wry look; Irini's English was
wellnigh perfect.

Turning to Petros, Irini said, 'We will have to teach
Troy to speak Greek. I will start to teach him a few
words tomorrow.'

'That's a good idea,' Petros started. 'You
can——'

'I think it's a good idea, too,' Laurel chimed in.
'But I wouldn't dream of troubling Irini. Surely it
would be too upsetting for her?'

That left them both without anything to say, and
Laurel quickly changed the subject. 'Is the boat we
came over to the island on named after you?'

'Yes,' Irini answered with some pride. 'It was a
wedding present to us from Niko's father.'

'It's beautiful,' Laurel said sincerely.

They started talking about boats then and the
subject, with Ross's help, occupied them until the meal
was finished. They had coffee in the sitting-room, but
almost immediately afterwards Laurel got to her feet.
'If you'll excuse me, I have to check on Troy.'

The boy was fast asleep, unaware of Laurel and of the woman who had gazed down at him and seen her dead husband's face in his. When she'd tucked him in, Laurel found her coat and went into the breakfast-room to let herself out on to the terrace. The night was very dark, very empty, without even any stars to lighten it. A breeze caught at her hair and lifted it, and carried on it came the scents from the garden, musky and sweet, a perfume that must be as old as the land itself. Going down the steps into the garden, Laurel walked along the lamp-lit paths, following the sound of water until she came to the fountain where she had sat with Ross earlier that day. She sat again on the stone bench, letting the scents and the time-lessness of Greece invade her senses all over again.

She didn't have long to wait. Ross walked along the path with confident steps, knowing where she would be. His jacket was open, his hands in his pockets. But when he reached her he didn't immediately come over to sit beside her, instead sitting on the edge of the fountain, facing her, so that the light that lit the cas-cading water was behind him, making it difficult to see his features. But he, of course, could see her per-fectly well.

'So what do you want to know about first? Although I bet I can guess.'

'Can you?'

'Yes; you want to know about Irini.'

'Yes,' Laurel acknowledged with a small smile.

'She's twenty-four, she comes from a rich Athenian family, and she and Niko were married for only about eight months before he was killed. Is that enough or do you want to know more?'

'Of course I do; you haven't yet told me the most important thing.'

He raised an eyebrow. 'And that is?'

'Did she love Niko? Was he in love with her?'

Ross tilted his head to look at her. 'Why is it so important to you? Are you—jealous?'

'Jealous?' Laurel shook her head. 'No, I'm not, strangely enough. My love for Niko faded away a long time ago. The time we had together was complete in itself, and since Troy has been born I've been too busy earning a living to worry about what might have been.'

'Irini would like you to be jealous of her. She thinks you ought to be.'

'I rather gathered that. But you haven't told me whether they were in love.'

'They'd known each other most of their lives. They got on all right and it was always understood that they would marry one day. The day would have been a whole lot sooner if Niko hadn't met you, I think. He rebelled against marriage for several years after that.'

'Really?' Laurel looked at Ross with some scepticism. 'You told me yourself that I wasn't the first girl he'd got into trouble.'

'No, but you *were* the first girl who mattered to him. Niko came the closest to rebelling that he'd ever done over you. If you hadn't refused completely to have an abortion, I think he would have gradually won Petros round to accepting you and would have been able to marry you. But your insistence on having Troy forced Niko's hand; he wasn't strong enough to stand up to Petros at that stage. You asked for more than he could give.'

Laurel was silent for a moment, thinking of what might have been if she had done as Niko wanted. But then she wouldn't have had Troy, and she found that her love for her son was far greater than anything she had felt for his father. So her voice was untroubled as she said, 'So presumably Niko went off and sowed a whole lot more wild oats until he married Irini. Did he—did he have any more illegitimate children?'

Ross shook his head. 'No, there's only Troy.' He paused for a moment. 'And to finally answer your question: no, I don't think he was *in love* with Irini, but he was ready to love her as his wife and the mother of his children. To be a good husband, in other words.'

'And Irini?'

'She had always known that one day she would marry him, so it didn't much matter whether she loved him or not. But yes, I think she cared for Niko, but only tenderly; it was no grand passion.'

A grand passion, Laurel thought. She had never thought of her affair with Niko in those terms before, but she supposed it could have been called that. Were all grand passions short-lived? Was love on that level too difficult to sustain, and did it then become the tender affection that Ross had descried for Niko and Irini? It seemed very sad if that was the case.

His eyes fixed on her pensive face, Ross said, 'What are you thinking?'

'That life doesn't come up to expectations.'

'Sometimes it does.'

Laurel gave a short laugh. 'Not in my experience, it doesn't.' She glanced across at him, wishing she could see his face properly. 'Perhaps you've been luckier.'

'In life—or in love?'

She shrugged, suddenly feeling avid with curiosity but trying to appear casual. 'Both.'

Ross stood up and went to lean with his back to the branch of a tree, his hands in his pockets again. 'I suppose luck in life starts right at the very beginning with your parents. There isn't much you can do about them, so you just have to thank your stars if you were born into a happy, settled, but stimulating environment.'

'And were you?'

'It was certainly stimulating,' Ross answered on a note of heavy cynicism. 'But always unsettled and seldom happy—except when I came here, to Temenos.'

'Your family connection goes back that far?'

'Oh, yes.' Again there was cynicism in his voice. 'I've known Petros all my life.' She could see his face more clearly now and thought she saw bleakness in his eyes, the twist of his mouth. Abruptly he straightened up and came over to sit beside her. 'Irini would like to make you jealous but you've no need to be; Niko never felt a fraction of what he felt for you for her. But what you've got to watch is that Irini doesn't start taking over Troy. Petros would like her to do that. Ideally, he would like you to hand the boy over to him and let him and Irini bring him up between them.'

With a gasp of horror, Laurel said, 'But surely Irini wouldn't want to bring up Niko's son by another woman?'

'Why not? Stranger things have happened. And she's under her parents' and Petros's thumb. She's a good Greek girl who will do as she's told; at least until Troy is old enough to go away to school. Then she'll probably be free to choose another husband.'

'But that's—that's horrible.' Laurel got agitatedly to her feet. 'And there's no way they're going to take Troy away from me. I'll leave here tomorrow. I should never have come. I should never have listened to you,' she said bitterly.

Ross reached to take hold of her wrist and pulled her down again. 'Simmer down! I said "ideally". Petros has already realised that you're not the push-over he would have liked. He respects you now. He may even come round to think that you're worthy to be the mother of his grandchild and ask you to stay on here with the boy.'

'You mean he'll have me along if he can't get Troy any other way,' Laurel said angrily.

'Put bluntly, yes. But if you don't want Petros to use you, then use him instead. It can be done, you know.'

Laurel gave him a curious glance. 'You're not afraid of Mr Alexiakis, are you?'

He looked surprised. 'No, of course not. Why should I be?'

'He's your employer, or at least your client, even though he is a family friend. But you don't even treat him with—with respect. You seem to enjoy needling him, making him angry.'

Ross's mouth twisted into a one-sided grin. 'You're very observant.' But he didn't enlighten her, instead saying rather abruptly, 'Is there anything else you want to know?'

There were a great many things. Laurel was fully aware that Ross had neatly ducked telling her anything about his love-life, and she would have liked to know whether he was married, for a start, but that was a question you just didn't ask because it was a dead giveaway. And she wanted to know what the connection was between him and Petros, and why they seemed to dislike one another so much, but those, too, were questions it wouldn't be wise to ask. So, instead, Laurel said, 'Yes. Who do all the clothes in my room belong to?'

'Haven't you been told? They are for you, of course.'

Laurel's mouth dropped open. 'For me? But they can't possibly be. You must be mistaken.'

'Hardly. I chose them for you myself.'

She stared at him speechlessly, her imagination filled with the picture of him going into stores, choosing all those beautiful clothes with her in mind. And those silky under-things, too; there were lots of those. She felt a flush of colour creeping up her cheeks and was glad of the darkness that hid it. But then it occurred to her that, although it might have been Ross who had chosen them, he was hardly likely to be the man who had paid the bill. 'I suppose Mr Alexiakis asked you to get them?' she said stiffly.

Warned by the note in her voice, Ross gave her a considering look. 'It occurred to us that you wouldn't be able to bring much with you and that you might like a few summer things to wear.'

'Is Mr Alexiakis in the habit of buying wardrobes of clothes for every woman who comes to stay here?'

'If he feels like it,' Ross answered easily. 'It's no big deal, Laurel. He's very rich and he likes to give people presents, especially women. He orders gold bracelets and watches by the dozen.'

If that remark was meant to give her comfort, it failed completely. 'I couldn't possibly wear them,' she said shortly. 'It would—compromise me.'

To her annoyance Ross laughed. 'How pompous
you sound.' Leaning forward he cupped her chin in
his hand. 'My darling girl, wear them, enjoy them.
Don't fight Petros, disarm him. Let him see what an
asset you would be to him, what a marvellous mother
you are to his grandson. Use your femininity to
capture him, the same way you captured Niko.'

Slightly thrown by his calling her his darling, even
though he did so very flippantly, and even more un-
nerved by the warmth of his hand, Laurel nevertheless didn't like the idea of such cold-bloodedness.
'I didn't set out to capture Niko, as you call it,' she
said quickly. 'It just happened.'

His fingers tightened for a moment on her chin as
Ross looked into her eyes. 'Yes,' he said softly. 'These
things do.' And then he leant forward to kiss her. It
was a lingering kiss of exploration, his lips taking hers,
liking what they found, and drinking deeply of her
youth and freshness. Laurel stiffened at first, taken
aback by surprise, but then she slowly relaxed, her
mouth opening under his on a long sigh of pleasure.

It was a while before Ross drew back. Laurel slowly
opened her eyes and found that he was watching her
closely, a strange, almost mocking look in his eyes.
She immediately thought that he had been testing her
in some way and quickly drew back, pushing his hand
away. 'Why did you do that?' she said in distress.

'Because I wanted to. Because I've wanted to for a
very long time.'

There was sincerity in his voice, but she was still
unsure. 'Really? Or is it because you find it amusing
to see if I'm—I'm available?'

His eyes looked steadily into hers. 'And are you
available?'

'No!'

'So now we know where we stand, don't we?'

Laurel didn't; she had no idea where she stood with him, but she knew that she had liked that kiss, liked it too much. She got quickly to her feet and went to walk away, but Ross caught up with her in one stride and swung her round to face him. 'Don't be silly,' he said shortly, and pulled her into his arms to kiss her again. This time it wasn't just a passing kiss; this time there was desire in the way his shoulders hunched and he held her against him, her softness against the lean length of his body. Laurel gasped, and for a few moments struggled in his hold, but his lips were hard and demanding, compelling her to submit. And it had been such a long, long time since she had been held in a man's arms.

She gave a small cry against his mouth and then her arms went round his neck as she let go the last remnants of resistance. Immediately the world began to whirl around her; she felt as if she was falling down some incredibly long spiralling cloud to some bright and beautiful place. Her head swam, and sensations deep in her body that she had held under rigid control for five long years seemed to burst into burning, hungry life. A great tremor of awareness ran through her and Laurel moaned, her body on fire with need. Ross's kiss deepened, but when she shuddered again he lifted his head to look down at her face in the moonlight. Her eyes were dark pools of longing, her lips parted and raised, eager for another embrace.

'How long is it since you were last kissed?' he asked softly.

His arms were still round her and she leant against him. Briefly she thought of the men in some of the places where she'd worked who had tried to kiss her, but that had only been lust and not what he meant. 'There hasn't been anyone since Niko,' she said simply.

'But you're so beautiful. So ripe for love.' As he spoke, Ross rained little kisses on her eyes, her cheeks, and then down the long, graceful column of her neck.

'Ross?'

But he put his finger against her lips and then replaced it with his mouth. When he raised his head at last Laurel's legs felt so weak that she had to cling to him as he turned and began to walk back to the house. Her thoughts became chaotic then. She was sure that Ross was taking her back to her room, or his room, sure that he meant to take their fervent embrace to its natural conclusion. But it was too soon, too much. Her body might be crying out for love but her whirling brain was desperately trying to send out danger signals. This isn't right. You don't know this man. You don't love him. But, oh, lord, I love what he was doing to me!

They went inside the house and Ross let her go while he closed the french doors and turned off the outside lights. Laurel took a deep breath to tell him that this was as far as he went, but then he had taken her hand to lead her through the quiet house to her room. Her heart was pounding like crazy and she was too agitated to speak as they stole like secret lovers through the quiet house. When they reached the corridor outside her room, Ross leant Laurel back against the wall to kiss her again and afterwards looked down into her half eager, half frightened, but wholly fascinated green eyes. He smiled, and again there was mockery in the twist of his mouth, but she saw now that the mockery was against himself. Reaching past her, he turned the knob of her door and pushed it open. Then he said, 'Goodnight, Laurel,' and turned to walk away.

CHAPTER SIX

YEARS of having to get up early made Laurel wake at
seven as usual the next morning, but she wished she
hadn't. It had been very late before she had finally
got to sleep and she still felt very tired. She glanced
at the other pillow and saw that Troy was still asleep,
curled into a small ball and with his teddy bear
clutched in his arms. She had found him there when
she had come into her room last night, lying awake
and nervously waiting for her. The child had never
had a room of his own before and had come looking
for her when he'd woken up in the night. At the time
Laurel had felt profound relief that Ross hadn't come
into the room with her, but now she lay and wondered
what had made him leave her at her door. And, even
more, she wondered if she would have had the strength
to turn him away if the initiative hadn't been taken
from her.

But Ross was too much of an enigma, and right
now her poor, tired brain felt unable to cope. She lay
in the big, comfortable bed and looked round the
room, taking in its richness all over again. Her eyes
lingered on the wardrobes that contained the clothes
she now knew were intended for her. *Should* she wear
them? She remembered a gorgeous pair of culottes
with a matching top and sash. But no, wearing those
clothes was going a lot further than meeting Petros
halfway; it would put her under an obligation to him
instead of the other way round. And you could hardly

tell a man to go to hell, if things went wrong, when you were wearing the clothes he'd paid for. No, she definitely couldn't allow her integrity to be compromised in that way. Although the things *were* beautiful. For a moment her skin yearned for the touch of silk almost as much as it had for Ross's touch last night. A blush of colour rose in her face, but then Laurel felt a great wave of mortification at her own weakness. Ross must think her very cheap, very easy. But this was followed by anger. Ross knew of her affair with Niko, none better, and he must have decided to try his luck with her, probably guessing that she was so frustrated that she would be an easy conquest. Which was true, she thought with bitter humiliation. But, if that was so, why had he walked away? It was something she had lain awake puzzling over last night, and the morning had brought no solution. All Laurel could think of was that she had been too easy, too eager; there had been no challenge for him and he had become bored.

This thought brought bitter shame, but Laurel wasn't the type who went in for self-flagellation, and she soon made up her mind to hold Ross at a long, cold distance in future. Which was a shame, because she had come to value his advice, although she wondered now if that had been entirely altruistic. Oh, hell, she didn't know what to think. Pushing the covers aside, Laurel went to the window and pulled back the curtains. The sun was rising against the deep blue of the sky, bringing that brilliantly clear light that Laurel had only ever found in Greece. At least she was here, and being in Greece felt like coming home.

Petros and Ross found the two of them having a great time in the indoor pool when they came down for a pre-breakfast swim around eight o'clock. Laurel was surprised to see the two men together and apparently on reasonable terms. Looking at them in just their bathing shorts, she was again struck by their similarities and differences. Petros's solid body had a great deal of dark, curling hair, while Ross was tall and fair, his body sleek and his chest hairless. But both men had wide, powerful shoulders and strong legs. If it came to a fight, Laurel wondered which one would win. But it had to be Ross, of course, because he was so much younger than Petros. And both men were handsome in their way, but Petros's handsomeness was of the rugged type that would soon disappear as his face became more fleshy; Ross, though, had the type of clean-cut good looks that would never fade. Watching them, as they walked down the length of the pool towards her, Laurel wondered again about that 'family connection'.

'Good morning.' It was Petros who spoke first. 'I hope you spent a comfortable night?'

'Yes, thank you.' Turning to Troy, who had his arms round her neck, she whispered, 'Say good morning to him in Greek.'

'*Kalimera,*' he said obediently.

Petros gave a guffaw of pleasure and jumped into the pool beside them. 'Can you swim, boy?' And when Troy shook his head, Petros held out his arms. 'Come, I teach you.'

Troy went willingly enough, and Laurel pretended to watch them, but out of the corner of her eye she saw Ross go to the diving-board and do a very neat dive into the deep end. He swam the length of the pool in a strong, easy crawl and emerged beside her, flicking the water from his hair. 'Good morning,

Laurel.' He began to smile at her but the smile faded
when she kept her face turned away and returned only
a cold greeting. His eyes went over her stony face and
to her fury his mouth creased into a wide grin of pure
amusement. 'Ah, I see.'

'See what?' she couldn't resist asking.

'That you've decided to be outraged.'

Laurel glared at him. 'I have every reason to be
angry.'

He dumbfounded her by immediately saying, 'Of
course you have.' But then he leant close to her ear
and, putting a familiar hand on her waist, said, 'But
I wonder why you weren't last night.' Then he laughed
aloud at the consternation in her face before turning
to swim away.

As a teenager Laurel had been quite a good
swimmer, but since she'd had Troy there had been
little chance to practise and it took her a while to get
back into the element. Now that Petros had taken
charge of Troy she was able to swim a few lengths
before going to check that her son was OK. But
grandfather and grandson were obviously enjoying
themselves and didn't need her. Turning on her back,
she began to swim lazily along, her hair floating free
around her head.

'You look like a water nymph,' Ross remarked,
coming alongside her.

He put his hand in her hair, letting it float through
his fingers, but Laurel quickly stood up and was glad
that she'd done so when she saw Irini push open the
door and walk into the pool area. Swimming across
to the steps, Laurel climbed out, sleeking her hair back
with her hands. 'Good morning, Irini.'

'Good morning.' Irini's eyes ran over her tall, slim figure in the old bathing suit that Laurel had had since her previous visit to Greece before Troy was born. But the jealousy that sharpened the other girl's features showed that she still looked good in it. 'Am I to have breakfast alone?' Irini said in Greek, addressing the men.

Laurel saw Petros frown, but he remembered his duty as a host and said to Troy, 'We will have another lesson tomorrow, huh?'

'Yes, please.' Troy crowed with laughter as Petros swam with him on his back across to the side, where Laurel lifted him out.

'We will all have breakfast,' Petros announced, and, putting on his robe, strode away to change.

Laurel put on her own robe and wrapped Troy in a towel. At the door she glanced back, expecting Ross to have got out, but he was swimming to the far end of the pool where Irini was standing. The water made sounds echo, and although Irini spoke in quite a low tone Laurel plainly heard her say in Greek, 'Where did you go last night, Stavros? I waited for you.' Not waiting to hear any more, Laurel quickly took Troy away.

After breakfast they all piled into Petros's German estate car and he drove them across the island to the ancient site. The men sat in the front and the girls and Troy behind. The centre of the island dipped away from the cliffs, like a giant fertile bowl. Much of it was cultivated, but the ground that wasn't was rich with wild flowers, the edges of the road thick with poppies. Wild orchids grew low among the grass and pink oleanders on the edge of the shallow river that meandered along the valley floor.

At the other side of the island there had once been an ancient port, built over many times and eventually destroyed by an earthquake a few hundred years ago. It had once been a thriving place but now there was only a small village of fifty or so houses and a couple of shops and tavernas. Leaving the car in the village, they followed Petros along a cobbled road that soon became no more than a track that wound through the pine trees and rose in steep zigzags up the hillside. They passed some ruins that had once been a sanctuary of Dionysus, and then came to an old, shaded theatre. As ancient Greek theatres went it was very small, the tiered seats uneven and overgrown, but there could be few places in the world in such a beautiful setting, overlooking the sea.

Laurel was wearing jeans and a thin sweater and found the going easy. Petros was helping Troy when he needed it and giving a running commentary to Laurel as he walked along. Ross, and Irini in her black dress and shoes too smart to be suitable for this kind of walking, were following more slowly. When they reached the theatre Petros took Troy to look out over the sea, but Laurel climbed the tiers of seats and sat up near the top, letting the atmosphere fill her soul, as it always did whenever she visited a place like this. Putting her hands on the hot, once-polished marble of the seat, she wondered about the people who had sat in this same spot over three thousand years ago. Their lives must have been so different, and yet they had looked out over this same sea and felt the heat of the same sun.

Hearing their voices, Laurel glanced down and saw that Ross and Irini were coming up the last bend in the path. An oleander bush grew out of the bank above them, and Laurel saw Irini point to it and Ross obligingly reach up and pick one of the sprigs of flowers for her. Irini smiled as she took it from him and said something that made Ross laugh. A flash of jealousy so violent that it shocked her ran through Laurel's veins. She looked quickly away, her fingers tightening on the edge of the stone, her heart beating in her chest. Before they could see her, she climbed to the top of the theatre and found the path that rose beyond it, hidden among the pine trees. She waited there, leaning against a tree, trying to still her heart, to beat down the intense feeling of jealousy.

What the hell had she to be jealous about, for heaven's sake? So the man had kissed her a couple of times; that certainly didn't mean anything. And she would be a fool if she let herself believe it did. Ross was obviously the type who enjoyed making a pass at a girl. The Greeks had a name for it: *kamaki*, the young men who preyed on girls, mostly tourists, with the one aim of getting them into bed and having a higher 'score' than their friends. But the next second she was telling herself how stupid that generalisation was; Ross wasn't Greek for a start, and he certainly hadn't taken her to bed last night. Nor Irini, from the sound of it, although the other girl had waited for him. Had he decided to leave her and go to Irini last night, but found that he was too late? Maybe he thought I was so besotted that I'd keep for another night, Laurel thought bitterly. He certainly seemed to be giving Irini all his attention today. Again jealousy burned her soul, and it came to Laurel with a sick feeling of despair that if she could feel this jealous then she must really care about Ross.

Petros and Troy joined her on the path and they climbed on up the hill, passing a tiny, comparatively modern chapel halfway up. At the top they found the ruins of an acropolis, the remains of some ancient walls built to guard the landward side of the port, and the inevitable temple of Athena. Laurel hadn't looked back once they had started the climb, and she was surprised to see that Ross was alone when he joined them.

'Where is Irini?' Petros demanded.

'She couldn't be bothered to walk all the way; she's waiting in the chapel.'

Petros nodded, and picked up Troy to show him the view. Ross sauntered over to where Laurel was standing, but she immediately averted her head and, turning away, went over to join the others. Ross watched her, his eyes narrowing.

'You see this stone,' Petros was saying to Troy. 'This writing is an oracle from Apollo at Delphi.'

'My Mummy has been to Delphi,' Troy informed him. 'She says it's the most beautiful place in the world. She went there with my Daddy.'

This artless remark caught at Petros's grief and his face worked as he tried to control it. To give him time to recover, Laurel went up to the stone and read out the inscription. '"I bid you announce to the people. Found now a city far-seen, in the Sea of Mists. I command so." It's still very clear. I wonder how long it has been here?'

'You read Greek very well,' Ross remarked, coming up behind her.

Laurel flushed, annoyed at giving herself away. 'I had to study ancient Greek at university. I remember a little.'

In control of himself again, Petros showed them what more there was to see and then they went back down the path. When they reached the chapel they found Irini inside, on her knees in front of the altar, apparently praying. It must have been a long prayer, Laurel thought cynically, and was immediately ashamed of herself. Perhaps Irini was religious; perhaps she derived comfort from it since Niko had died. But if she was still grieving why had she waited for Ross last night? Irini's prayers evidently pleased Petros, though; he nodded in approval when he saw her.

They all lunched at one of the tavernas down in the village, but Troy didn't eat very much of the strange food and grew tired, leaning against Laurel with his eyes drooping.

'The boy needs to rest,' Petros announced. 'We will go back.'

He lifted Troy up and carried him over to the car as Laurel followed, wondering whether Petros would ever call him anything except 'the boy'. When they reached the car she and Irini got in the back. Petros leaned in from the side nearest Irini and for a horrid moment Laurel thought he was going to give Troy to Irini to hold, but after only a fraction of a second's hesitation he very gently reached across and placed Troy in her own arms.

Laurel was glad to get back to the villa. She settled Troy down for his nap, took a shower, and then went in search of Thespina. On the way she passed the door to Petros's study and heard men's voices. Petros and Ross talking business, presumably. She couldn't distinguish any words and just hoped they weren't dis-

cussing her, although she wouldn't be surprised.
Nothing would surprise her in this place.

Thespina was in the kitchen, a big room with tiles
of burnt umber on the floor, a big cooking range
against one wall and bunches of herbs drying from
hooks in the ceiling. She was talking to another
woman, the cook presumably, but immediately turned
to Laurel.

'You need something, Miss Marland? I'm sorry, I
didn't hear you ring.'

'No, I didn't ring.' Laurel gave her a warm smile.
'I thought I'd come and talk to you myself about
meals for Troy. I'm afraid he isn't used to very rich
food. I thought perhaps we could work out a menu
for him.'

'But of course.'

Laurel was invited to sit down at the table on the
patio outside the kitchen, the cook made coffee and
came to join them, and between the three of them,
with Thespina acting as an unnecessary interpreter,
they devised meals that Troy would happily eat.
Afterwards the cook went back into her kitchen, but
Laurel kept Thespina with her by asking questions
about the house and the island, gently leading round
to the questions she really wanted to ask.

'I expect Mr Alexiakis has guests here all the time?'

'Not so much now, since Mr Niko died. Before that
the house was often full for weeks on end.'

'That must have meant a lot of work for you,'
Laurel said in genuine sympathy, remembering times
when she'd had to cater for a houseful of guests.

'Oh, yes.'

Thespina described some house parties with famous
names among the guests, and it was a little while

before Laurel could say casually, 'Mr Ashton was telling me that he's been coming here for years.'

The housekeeper nodded. 'Mr Stavros, yes, he often comes.'

'And does he ever bring his wife and family with him?'

With a surprised shake of her head, Thespina answered, 'Mr Stavros has no wife. He is—what do you call it?—a playboy. No, that's wrong; a bachelor, I should say.'

Right the first time, Laurel thought drily. 'I expect Irini—Madame Alexiakis is pleased to have his company; it must be very lonely for her here.'

'She does not often come. She has gone back to live with her family.'

There was withdrawal in Thespina's tone so Laurel didn't push it, instead talking of general things until a bell sounded and Thespina hurried away to answer it.

The afternoon sun was hot, almost like that of an English summer. Laurel wandered down to the open-air pool, found a lounger and lay down to catch up on some of her lost sleep.

She was awakened, in the best of traditions, by a kiss. It was a very light kiss that brushed her lips as gently as a butterfly's wings, but quite sufficient to wake her. Laurel opened her eyes, her heart suddenly pounding—and found *two* faces hovering over her. Those of Ross and Troy. Both of them bore big, conspiratorial grins, making her wonder who had given her the kiss. Not Troy, she thought; his kisses were usually more robust than that. Ross was crouching down, holding the boy round the waist, and Troy had a confident arm round his neck.

'Your son was looking for you,' Ross advised her. 'I told him we'd probably find you lazing around somewhere.' Taking her hand, he pulled Laurel to her feet. 'Come on, lazy-bones. We want to go down to the beach.'

'Yes, come on lazy-bones.'

Troy took her other hand and between them they pulled her along, giving Laurel no chance to stand on her pride where Ross was concerned.

There was a path leading down from the garden to the beach, sometimes with steps cut into the rock surface on the steepest parts. The beach was bigger than she'd expected and was mostly shingle, but at one end there was a cave that went deep into the cliff, and in front of this there was a wide strip of clean yellow sand. 'Perfect for making sand-castles!' Laurel exclaimed.

But then wished she hadn't when Troy said in disappointment, 'But I haven't got a bucket and spade.'

'Never mind,' Ross said firmly. 'We'll make one with our hands. Come on.' Still holding Laurel's hand, he led them to the water's edge where the sand was still damp. 'You can find some shells.'

'Yes, Mummy, you find some shells,' Troy repeated importantly.

Laurel put her hands on her hips. 'Men!' she exclaimed indignantly, making Troy peal with laughter.

Soon they were all busily working to create a castle. Ross and Troy chatted away as it grew quickly under their combined efforts, and Laurel was intrigued to hear Troy getting lessons in medieval warfare, civil engineering, and the history of the Knights Templars as it was being built. She had been pressing her collection of shells into the ramparts, the knees of her trousers getting wet in the process, then sat back on the dry sand to admire their work. Watching them adding yet another tower to the retaining wall, Laurel thought: this is what it must be like to be a family. Sharing, being together and having time for each other, the child learning from its parents. She wondered if Niko would have made a good father. She supposed he would, but somehow Niko wasn't in her thoughts very much, even though they were on his island. It was as if, now she had said goodbye to him at his grave, he was only a memory. Now, she realised, her thoughts were full only of Ross.

'Hey, there! Wake up.' She became aware that Ross was calling her. 'We need some more shells.'

'Big ones, Mummy,' Troy added, without looking at her.

Ross grinned at Laurel and, hoisting himself to his feet, came over to her. 'I wonder what you were thinking about with that dreamy expression in your eyes and that little half-smile on your lips,' he said softly.

'As a matter of fact I was thinking about Niko,' she said half truthfully, but couldn't stop the little flush of colour that crept into her cheeks.

'Ah, of course.' But she knew that he didn't believe her.

They began to walk along the beach together, their feet bare, Ross keeping a firm hold of her hand. 'What's Irini doing this afternoon?' Laurel said stiffly.

'Resting, I should imagine. She does quite a bit of resting when she's here.'

Her curiosity getting the better of her, Laurel asked, 'Was she with Niko when he was killed?'

'No. She isn't such a good skier as Niko was. She was down on the lower slopes when the avalanche came down.'

'She must have been terribly upset,' Laurel said with sincere sympathy. 'And Mr Alexiakis too, of course. It must have been dreadful for him.'

'Yes, it wasn't pleasant having to break the news to him,' Ross agreed grimly.

'You told him?' Laurel's eyes widened.

'No one else would do it.' Ross gave a short laugh. 'On the assumption that the bearer of bad tidings gets his head cut off.'

'Mr Alexiakis ought to be grateful.'

This time there was real amusement in Ross's laugh. 'Petros be grateful to me! He'd rather die.'

Frowning, Laurel said, 'But why? I don't understand. You seem to dislike each other so much at times. And yet at other times...' She shrugged in perplexity.

'Put it down to the Greek temperament,' Ross said cheerfully, and bent to pick up a large shell poking up from the sand.

'But you're not Greek.'

Instead of answering, Ross took the shell to the sea where he washed it clean of sand and then shook it dry. 'Do you hear anything?' he asked, holding it against her ear.

She looked into his eyes. 'All I hear is the sea, the real sea.'

'And no substitute will do for the real thing, is that it?'

She nodded slowly, wondering what he was thinking.

It immediately became clear when Ross took the shell away and looked down at it in his hands, as if studying intently its rich pink lustre. 'If it's any comfort to you, your photograph was in Niko's wallet when he died. I found it there.' Then he turned and threw the shell far out to sea with all the force of his arm.

'That's—nice to know.'

He turned to look at her, his eyes intent on her face. 'Nice? Is that all?'

Laurel licked lips that had gone suddenly dry, realising that this moment was important, and that pride and coyness had no place here. 'Yes, that's all. When I was thinking of Niko back there, it was— well, it was because I'd realised how much his memory had faded. He's part of my past now.'

With tension behind apparent casualness, Ross said, 'And did you also think it might be time to start thinking about the future?'

But that was going too far. Turning away, Laurel said primly, 'Troy is my future.'

He laughed then, the old mockery back in his voice. 'Of course. What other interests could a young, beautiful woman have than bringing up her son all alone?'

She shot him a fiery glance, but then gave an exclamation as an extra-large wave took them by surprise and came halfway up to their knees, showering them with spray. 'Oh, our trousers are soaked.'

'So they are.' Ross gave her a grin of pure devilment. 'I'll take mine off to dry if you will.'

'Oh, Ross! Of all the corny remarks. I don't want to...' Her voice faded as he put his arm round her waist and drew her to him.

'What don't you want?' He looked down into her eyes, arrogant amusement in his face.

'I don't want to know you,' she managed.

'What a delightful little liar you are,' he said, his eyes darkening, and put his other arm round her to hold her close against him.

'No, Ross, please. Not in front of Troy.'

'He would soon get used to it.' And he brushed her cheek with his lips, leaving Laurel in no doubt about whose kiss had awakened her earlier.

His words excited her, making promises as they did for the future, but still she held back. 'He's so little. He wouldn't understand. And he might—he might say something in front of the others.'

Ross's eyes narrowed. 'And that would upset you?'

'Yes, it would.' Laurel's voice hardened a little. 'Wouldn't it upset you if Irini knew the game you were playing?'

'Game?' The laughter left his face. 'Is that what you think this is?'

'Isn't it?' She waited eagerly for his reassurance.

Letting her go, Ross said lightly, 'But of course. Isn't all life a game? And especially love.' He glanced back. 'I think your son is waiting for his shells.'

Miserable, knowing that she had spoiled things, Laurel said, 'You threw the best one away.'

He nodded, his mouth twisting ruefully. 'So I did. Never mind, there are thousands more shells on the beach. Aren't there, Laurel?' he added tauntingly, and strode off without waiting for her.

It was Petros who was in a good mood at dinner that night, although he frowned when he saw that Laurel was wearing the same dress as the night before. 'You said she would need a new wardrobe of clothes,' he said to Ross in Greek. 'Why does she not wear them?'

'She is too proud.'

'It is not polite to refuse a gift.' But Petros treated her with courtesy, her stock evidently having gone up when he found out that she knew as much as he did about his ancient ancestors. They began to discuss the Greek myths and legends, but Irini looked bored and turned to Ross for entertainment. But he seemed preoccupied tonight and he drank more than usual, his eyes glittering as he watched Laurel over the rim of his wine glass. Becoming aware that one of his guests was being neglected, Petros turned to Irini. 'What would you like to do tomorrow, my dear?'

Irini shrugged. 'Go sailing, perhaps.'

'That's a marvellous idea. I've promised Troy that I will teach him to fish. We'll take out a caique and go to——'

'I didn't mean sail in a fishing boat,' Irini said in horror. 'I meant go out in the ocean cruiser.'

Petros looked disappointed, but said, 'Of course. Just as you wish. Where would you like to go.'

'To Santorini, perhaps.'

'Santorini?' Laurel looked up in excitement. 'That's the island that was supposed to be Atlantis, isn't it? I've always wanted to go there.'

'Then Santorini it is,' Petros said, pleased that she was keen to go. 'I will instruct Captain Andreas to have the boat ready early tomorrow morning.'

After dinner they had coffee in the big sitting-room as before, but tonight Laurel made no attempt to go into the garden. She went to her room at about eleven and lay awake wondering if Ross had gone to Irini.

They were up early for breakfast the next morning, both Laurel and Troy eager for the projected trip to Santorini. Petros brought the car round himself, but it was Irini who sat next to him in the passenger-seat. Laurel's heart did a crazy little jump as she thought that Ross was going to sit in the back with them, but instead he came up to close the door. 'Have a good day,' he said to them.

Immediate disappointment showed on Troy's face while Laurel tried hard to disguise her own. 'Aren't you coming?'

He shook his head. 'I have things to do here.'

'Please come with us,' Troy said, reaching out to him.

'Sorry, old son, but I can't today. But I wonder if you would do something for me?' He fished in his pocket and took out some money which he gave to Troy. 'Would you buy me a bucket and spade so that I can help you make another sand-castle? And will you buy an ice-cream for your mummy and for yourself?'

Troy gravely agreed to do as he asked, and put in that way it was impossible for Laurel to object.

Ross waved them off and Laurel sat back in the car, her eagerness for the trip suddenly greatly deflated. It wouldn't be the same without him. She looked at the back of Petros's and Irini's heads, thinking that she would have to spend every day with just them for company if Ross hadn't been there. The prospect was rather a daunting one, although she hadn't expected Ross to come to Temenos with them. Laurel realised that she had been using Ross as a buffer, as a confidant, someone she could turn to if she felt lonely or alien.

Captain Andreas was waiting for them with his usual big smile and they made good progress through the calm seas to Santorini, where they anchored in the lagoon created by the long ago earthquake that had devastated the island. The harbour now lay at the bottom of very steep cliffs with the town of Thera at the top. There were two ways up, by cable-car or by mule. Troy was given the choice and after a few torn moments opted for the mules.

'Laurel and I will take the cable-car,' Irini announced.

That suited Petros but it didn't suit Laurel, who would have loved to see her son's excitement at his first ever ride on a mule. But she generously decided to let Petros have that pleasure to himself and went with Irini.

The town was full of tourist shops, catering for the many cruise ships which came to the island for a few hours before moving on. Most of them were jewellery shops at which Irini lingered, but Laurel was eager to get to the head of the zigzag road that the mules took, to meet Troy. So she hurried ahead and laughed with delight when she saw them coming, her son sitting on the poor animal with a huge smile of pleasure on his face. Troy bought the bucket and spade for Ross, taking some time to choose a really nice one. He and Laurel went into the shop alone so that they were able to speak Greek, which so amazed the shopkeeper that Troy came out with a big bag of sweets as a present.

Lunch was eaten at a restaurant that clung to the side of the cliff and gave a most magnificent view over the lagoon far below. The scenery was beautiful, the food good, but Laurel found that she missed having Ross there to share it with. After lunch Petros

took Troy back to the boat to teach him to fish, he
said, but Laurel was obviously expected to want to
go round the shops with Irini. She demurred, but
Petros mistook her reasons and took Laurel to one
side and tried to press a wad of drachmas into her
hand. 'You buy some things for yourself, for the boy,'
he urged.

But Laurel drew back, her face hot. 'Oh, no, please.
I couldn't.'

But Petros insisted. 'You buy something nice.
Come, you take it. It is what Niko would want.'

Laurel had to take the money because to make a
scene by refusing more forcefully would have been
undignified, though Petros made things easier by
giving Irini some money, too. But Laurel didn't spend
any of hers, and was uncomfortably aware of the
money in her handbag the whole time. Irini, of course,
spent hers without a qualm, and kept trying to persuade Laurel into buying things. 'Look, this blouse
would suit you.' Or, 'Why don't you buy a bracelet
as a souvenir?' And eventually got angry when Laurel
kept saying no. 'My father-in-law has given you this
money. Why do you not spend it?'

'I can't. It wouldn't be right.'

'That is ridiculous. He will be unhappy if you don't.
I do not understand you.'

Laurel looked at her steadily. 'Yes, you do, Irini.
You're Greek. And you know the circumstances.
You're family, I'm not.'

'But you want to be family. Why else did you come
here?'

'So that Troy would have the chance to see his
father's country. We're here for a holiday, Irini, that's
all. I don't intend to stay here—or to let Troy stay

here without me,' Laurel said firmly. 'I don't want to cut you out with Mr Alexiakis, if that's what you're afraid of, Irini.'

'But even so you will let Petros leave all his money to the boy when he dies.'

'I can't stop him from doing what he wants with his own money,' Laurel replied. 'But I can make darn sure that he doesn't take us over. I don't want my son to be brought up the way Niko was. I want Troy to be free to make his own choices.'

'You want him to be free to choose his own wife, is that what you mean?' Irini said tartly.

'His own wife, his own career, his own country. Everyone should have that right, above family commitment.'

The other girl gave her a long, keen look, and then nodded—and smiled. She looked a whole lot nicer when she smiled. 'I believe you. I, too, think everyone should be free to choose for themselves.' She smiled again. 'But Petros will still be offended if you give him back the money.'

They solved that problem by finding a church and putting the wad of notes in the offertory box. And then Irini completely surprised Laurel by going into a jewellery shop and coming out with a gold bracelet which she fastened on Laurel's wrist. 'This is a present from me and you cannot refuse.'

'But I have nothing to give you,' Laurel said in some distress.

'You have given me more than you realise.' Her eyes shone and, for the first time since she'd met her, Irini looked happy.

Ross wasn't around when they got back to Temenos, but when Laurel went into the sitting-room before dinner he was there alone. He was standing at the bar pouring a drink and glanced round when she came in. There was a tremulous smile on Laurel's lips, but it faded when she saw his face harden. Slamming down the bottle he was holding, he came striding over to her, caught her wrist and pulled her after him back through the door, all without a word.

'Hey! Wait a minute!' Laurel exclaimed indignantly.

But Ross marched along, dragging her behind him until they came to her room. Opening the door, he pulled her inside and closed it behind them.

'Just what is this?' she demanded in stunned bewilderment.

'You,' he said forcefully, 'have worn that same dress every evening since you've been here. There is a whole wardrobe of dresses in there.' He gestured towards the dressing-room. 'Now go and put one on.'

Laurel gave a gasp of indignation. 'Just who the hell do you think you are, issuing orders? I shall dress exactly as I please.'

'Not in that dress, you won't.'

'Oh, no?' Her chin came up in determined defiance.

'No, because I shall tear the damn thing off you.'

Laurel's mouth dropped open. 'You wouldn't dare.' But even before she'd finished the sentence her voice had faded. Looking into his menacing grey eyes, she knew that he'd do exactly as he threatened.

'Wouldn't I?' He took a step towards her and reached out his hand.

'No.' She backed away, putting up her hands to hold him off. 'I'll scream. You'll frighten Troy.'

'Coward,' he said on a mocking sneer. 'Hiding behind your son.' He took another step towards her. 'Do you *want* me to tear it off?'

Laurel came up against the wall and gulped, her eyes huge in her face. 'All—all right. I—I'll change.'

'And not just the dress; put on the underwear I chose too.'

'Oh, now wait a minute. I——'

'You'll what?' Ross put one hand against the wall, the other on her shoulder.

'I'll—er—just go and change.' She slipped out from under his arm and ran to the dressing-room. At the door she paused to look back. Ross had turned and was watching her, feet apart, his hands on his hips, and his chin jutting forth in forceful determination.

She chose delicate creamy silk underwear and a dress the colour of faded pink roses to cover it. The dress had a full, swirling skirt and a low-cut bodice under a lace top and long sleeves. There were shoes to match, everything fitting perfectly. Laurel imagined Ross studying her figure to guess her size, letting the lace underwear run through his fingers as he chose it. He must be very experienced if he was that good at guessing, Laurel thought nervously. Pushing back the hair on one side of her head, she fastened it with a clip and went out into the bedroom.

Ross was still there, waiting to see if she had obeyed him, presumably. He had his back to her and caught sight of her reflection in a large, gold-framed mirror first. His shoulders tensed, then he turned slowly to face her, his eyes drinking her in. 'You look—very lovely,' he said in a strange, uneven kind of voice.

He held out his hand, and, as Laurel walked towards him and put her hand into his, she knew, beyond any shadow of doubt, that she had fallen in love with the wrong man all over again.

CHAPTER SEVEN

INWARDLY reeling from the shock of discovery, Laurel let Ross pick up her hand and kiss it. 'You have very good taste,' she said stiltedly. 'You must be used to buying clothes for women.' Her feelings in a whirl, the words were out before Laurel could stop them.

Ross immediately raised a sardonic eyebrow. 'Of course. I do it all the time.' Dropping her hand, he said, 'We'd better go; the others will be wondering where we are.'

That meal was the most pleasant Laurel had experienced at Temenos. Everyone seemed to be in a good mood, especially Irini, who laughed and smiled a lot. Petros saw Laurel's dress and the bracelet on her wrist and nodded approvingly, thinking that she had bought it with his money.

The delicious food and the wine added to Laurel's already heightened sense of anticipation. She was sitting opposite Ross and it was impossible to avoid his eyes. The sardonic look had gone and she seemed to read messages in them. 'Later. In the garden.' She imagined being held in his arms again, feeling his lips on hers, and her heart began to thud so loudly that she was sure everyone must hear it. She longed for the meal to end, and yet in some indefinable way wanted to prolong the exquisite pleasure of anticipation. But when they'd had coffee and she went to her bedroom to check on Troy she heard the patter of rain on the windows. Pulling back the curtains, she saw the first spatter of rain become heavier, beating against the panes. Then there was a rumble of thunder as a storm broke and lightning lit the sky.

'Mummy?' Troy was in her bed, sitting up and rubbing his eyes.

'It's all right, darling. It's only a storm.' She went quickly to him and put her arms round his small, solid body.

They made a game of counting the seconds from thunder to lightning, but soon a tap came at the door and Ross came in.

'Is everything all right?'

'Yes, fine. We're listening to the storm.'

Coming across to them, Ross sat on the bed on Troy's other side so that the child was between them. He gave Laurel a rueful look over the boy's head. 'The elements appear to be against us.'

He began telling Troy a story about a time when he had been out in a rowing-boat when he was young and a terrible storm had caught the boat before it could get back to shore. 'Your daddy was there, too,' he said. 'He was only about seven years old at the time. The sea kept coming into the boat and we had to bail like mad to try and get it out.'

Troy was listening, bug-eyed, so absorbed that he reverted to baby talk. 'Did you think you would be drownded?'

Ross nodded seriously. 'The sea was too rough to row so I took off my shirt and tied it to an oar and waved it, but no one could see it because of the waves.'

'What did you do?' It was Laurel who spoke, as fascinated as her son.

'We took all our clothes off, wrapped them in the sail and hoisted them to the top of the mast, then I set fire to them. And luckily your grandfather, and *his* father, were out in a big boat looking for us, and they saw the fire and came and rescued us.'

'I bet they were glad they found you,' Troy remarked, pleased with the happy ending.

A shadow flickered in Ross's eyes. 'Yes, but they were very angry with me for taking your daddy out in the boat with me.' Ross could have only been about fourteen himself, Laurel thought, and must have been scared to death, so it had been an incredibly brave thing to do. But Ross said briskly, 'And quite right too.' He stood up. 'I'll leave you to go back to sleep. And tomorrow we're all going to go on a picnic. Goodnight. Goodnight, Laurel. See you both tomorrow.'

Troy was fully awake and it was some time before he went to sleep again—still in Laurel's bed. The rain was still falling, and she knew that there was no chance of meeting Ross; but he had already told her that in his final goodnight. But there was tomorrow to look forward to and all the tomorrows after that. And tonight she could at least dream of Ross.

The island had a beautiful washed-clean appearance as they drove through it the next morning. And the rain had acted like a magic wand and carpeted every hillside with thousands more wild flowers in every colour of the rainbow. Captain Andreas had been invited along today, and they drove in the estate car to a sandy bay on the other side of the island, the vehicle rocking from side to side on the rough track, and having to be left about a hundred yards from the beach. Thespina had packed the food for them, and her idea of a picnic was a far cry from Laurel's and Troy's usual packet of sandwiches and a couple of cans of soft drink. There were two whole chickens and salad, vine-leaved *dolmathes*, little cheese pies called *tiropittakia*, bread and olives, lots of fruit, and bottles of wine and lemonade in a big cool-box.

Troy had never had it so good; he was over-whelmed by adults who were willing to play with him and help make sand-castles. Ross had brought his bucket and spade along and had also found a cricket bat and stumps. In the morning they changed into swim-suits, Laurel wearing a beautifully cut black one-piece that she'd found among the new clothes, and swam, then built a huge sand-castle. After lunch they all played cricket. Troy was the instructor in the game, gravely telling his grandfather and Captain Andreas the rules, and then he captained one side and Ross the other. As Ross could already play he was given Laurel and Irini on his side, which made him pull a very woebegone face.

'Chauvinist,' Laurel hissed at him as he told her where she was to field.

They didn't do too badly, considering neither girl had played before. Even Irini really entered into the spirit of the game, which surprised Laurel, and looked quite upset when she dropped a couple of catches. Their turn came to bat and Ross went in first, sending the fielders running, so that Troy made them stand close to the wicket to try and get a catch.

Laurel sat on the sand near the remains of their picnic and watched her son taking command in some amusement.

'Troy is enjoying himself,' Irini remarked.

Glancing at her, Laurel saw the happiness in the other girl's face, the lines of pettishness around her mouth completely gone. 'So are you. You seem so much more—relaxed.'

Irini nodded, and after a moment's hesitation said confidingly, 'It's because you said you would not let Troy stay in Greece without you. If you had been willing to leave him here I would have had to look after him for several years. It would have been my duty. But now I will be free to live my own life. I have married to please my family and now I will be able to please myself.' There was an unmistakable light in her eyes as she spoke and her mouth unknowingly curved into a soft smile.

'You look as if you have someone in mind,' Laurel said in surprise.

'Yes. Perhaps.' Irini looked across to where the men were all gathered round the wicket, Ross standing at the crease, Captain Andreas the wicket-keeper. Her whole face filled with yearning. 'I have been in love with him for a long time, but he wouldn't have been considered suitable, of course, so I had to put him out of my mind and out of my heart. But now that Niko is dead and I don't have to look after his child...' She shrugged expressively. 'Now I'm free to love as I please.'

Laurel had followed the direction of her glance and saw with a sick feeling of dread that she was watching Ross. 'And is this man—does he return your feelings?' she asked painfully.

'Oh, yes.' Irini positively glowed. 'But we couldn't say anything. It is too soon after Niko's death, not yet a year. And until I knew what you would do there was always the possibility that I wouldn't be really free for several years.'

'Out!' The excited shout came and Ross had no umpire to appeal to. 'You next, Mummy,' Troy called.

Laurel felt like crying, but turned her feelings into anger instead, and to her own and everyone else's amazement hit the ball so hard that she scored several sixes before being caught out by Captain Andreas.

'Who taught you to play?' Ross asked admiringly when she came to join him, Irini going in to bat.

'It was instinctive,' she said shortly. She had reason to be curt with him; if he had this understanding with Irini then what the hell had he been doing flirting with *her*?

Ross studied her set profile with a frown. His eyes went over her slim figure in the low-backed, high-cut swim-suit and he seemed to be considering something, then came to a decision. 'I shall be leaving here first thing tomorrow morning,' he said abruptly.

Her head jerked round and for a moment there was consternation in Laurel's large, vulnerable eyes. 'You—you're going away?'

'Yes. Back to London.'

'For how long?'

'I'm not sure.'

'Will you——?' Laurel tried hard to master her voice. 'Will you came back before Troy and I leave?'

'Do you want me to?' The question was direct, startling.

Laurel quickly turned away, her heart beating, her thoughts in a whirl of common sense against love. Yes, of *course* she wanted him to come back; she didn't want him to leave. But how could she possibly tell him so after Irini had confided the truth to her? But perhaps Irini had been wrong; perhaps it was only wishful thinking on her part and Ross didn't return her love. Or maybe he had been fond of the other girl but had changed his mind when he'd met Laurel again. In that case surely there was a chance for her own happiness? And by saying no now she might be ruining her one chance of winning it. Or perhaps Ross intended to marry Irini and wanted Laurel as his mistress; after all, she'd been Niko's mistress, hadn't she? He was waiting for her to answer and she didn't know what to say. She turned tortured eyes towards him. She had to have things out in the open. She had to *know* how he felt.

Opening her mouth, she went to ask the all-important question, but just then there came a great shout from the cricket players as Irini was bowled out. The others came running towards them and Ross reached out and gripped her wrist. 'Well?' he demanded, his eyes intent on hers.

Laurel shook her head helplessly. 'I—I just don't know.'

Ross's mouth tightened, his eyes blazed for an instant, but the next moment he let her go and stood up, lifting up Troy as he came up to them and saying, 'Well played. Well played.'

'But your team won,' Troy objected. 'It was Mummy hitting all those sixes.' His voice was torn between disappointment at losing and pride in his mother's prowess.

The rest of the day was hell. Laurel tried to pretend to be as cheerful as before, but it didn't really matter because everyone else seemed too happy to notice. Even Ross; but then Ross, she had found, was extremely good at hiding his feelings. He drove on the way back, with Petros as always in the front passenger-seat, while Laurel sat with Irini, and Troy and

Captain Andreas took the rear seats. Laurel wondered why Irini could stay so cheerful when she knew
that Ross was leaving, but then it turned out that she
didn't know, because when Ross announced at dinner
that he was leaving the next morning Irini looked
completely disconcerted.

'You're going to Athens from Naxos?' she asked.

'No, to London. There's no flight from Naxos
tomorrow, so I shall take the *Irini* to Piraeus and fly
from there.'

Laurel had to look away; she couldn't bear to watch
Irini's face as she struggled to hide her feelings, her
own heart full of understanding sympathy. 'Will you
be coming back soon?' Laurel's own question was
echoed in the Greek girl's voice.

'I'm not sure; I have some business in London to
sort out.'

'You may as well leave the boat in Piraeus until one
of us needs it,' Petros remarked. 'Andreas was telling
me that there are a few repairs needed; they can be
done in the boatyard there.'

Troy looked disappointed; he had enjoyed going on
the boat and he had developed an admiration for
Captain Andreas almost equal to that for Ross, having
confided to Laurel that he would like to be a sea-
captain when he grew up.

'If you're taking the boat to Athens I might as well
go along,' Irini was saying as artlessly as she could
manage. 'I would like to see my family.'

Petros frowned at her. 'You promised to keep Laurel
company,' he pointed out shortly.

Irini flushed and looked away, and Laurel didn't
say anything. With Ross leaving she certainly didn't
want to be here with just Petros and the servants for

adult company. Even Irini—as miserable as she would
probably be—would be better than that. And Laurel
was feminine enough to be glad that Ross and Irini
wouldn't have a day alone together on the boat.

After coffee had been drunk Ross and Petros went
off to the latter's study to talk business and Irini immediately went to her room. Laurel looked in on Troy
and found him for once still in his own bed, fast
asleep, worn out by what for him had been a wonderful day of little-known fun, when he had been the
centre of everyone's attention. Her own room was in
darkness and she left it that way as she went to the
window and pulled back the curtains. Tonight it was
dry and noticeably warmer, a bright moon lighting
the garden. Opening the window, Laurel leaned out.
From here she could see the path that led from the
terrace to the fountain, and then on down to the
beach. Would Ross go to the seat by the fountain when
he and Petros had finished their business talk? Would
he expect to find her waiting for him so that he could
again take her in his arms and kiss her until the world
spun giddily around them? Laurel didn't know, wasn't
sure. But suddenly it came to her that she had to take
the chance, that she would never be able to live with
herself in the future if she didn't at least try for happiness now.

Going quickly to the wardrobe, she pulled out a
jacket and put it on, then went over to close the
window, not wanting the room to get cold. She leaned
forward to reach the catch and noticed a movement
out in the moonlit garden. Ross going down to the
fountain already? Her heart jumped. But it was a
woman's figure, easily distinguishable in the pale grey
dress that Irini had worn at dinner. The Greek girl

had taken off her shoes, and ran lightly down the path, hurrying to meet her lover.

When she was out of sight, Laurel closed the window, drew the curtains, took off her jacket, which she carefully hung up in the wardrobe again, then went to bed wishing that she were dead.

Ross had gone by the time Laurel put in an appearance the next morning. She was glad of that; she hadn't wanted to see him. Petros had taken Troy off in a caique to give him another fishing lesson, so Laurel went down to the outside pool to sunbathe. Irini joined her there an hour or so later, her eyes dark-rimmed by tiredness. She must have had quite a night, Laurel thought bitterly. They exchanged greetings but then, by tacit consent, just sat and looked at magazines without saying much to each other, the thoughts of both girls on a boat sailing to Piraeus.

Luckily the weather over the next week was warm and sunny, so that the girls were able to spend most of the days sunbathing by the pool. They had little else to do; Petros took Troy out somewhere every day, showing him off with pride in the village, teaching him to sail and fish. Laurel and Irini would meet them at the little port after their expeditions and they would all have lunch in one of the tavernas, or go for a picnic on the beach. But there were many hours when the two girls were alone together, and a friendship began to grow between them, despite the circumstances. It fulfilled a need on Irini's side at first; she had been sent away to school and most of her friends were scattered throughout Europe, so that she had no one she could confide in. Laurel, too, had been without close friends since Troy was born, but she found it almost

impossible to be open with Irini because she knew
they were in love with the same man.

Laurel didn't know whether to be pleased or not
when Irini, sensing her reserve, thought it was because of Niko. So Irini carefully refrained from men-
tioning Niko's name and their friendship grew on a
superficial 'girl talk' level. They discussed clothes and
décor and films and music, and learnt quite a bit about
each other in the process. Their lifestyles were completely different, of course—Cinderella, before and
after the ball—but Irini was very envious of Laurel's
having Troy.

'I would like to have lots of children,' she confided
to Laurel.

'I'm sure you'd make a good mother,' Laurel replied stiltedly, trying not to picture the mixture of
children that Ross and Irini might have.

'Yes.' Irini sat back with satisfaction. 'He will give
me many little ones.' She rubbed her hands dreamily
down her stomach and legs, her mind full of sensuous
images.

'I think I'll have another swim.' Laurel dived into
the water and worked off her feelings of despair and
frustration by swimming vigorously up and down the
pool until she was too tired to go any further.

After breakfast one morning, when she had been
at Temenos for nearly two weeks, Petros asked her to
go into his study with him. He invited her to sit down,
but Laurel perched on the edge of the chair, her
shoulders braced, knowing what was coming.

Petros began to speak, his words obviously pre-
viously and carefully thought out, and in five minutes
offered her an entirely new life. A house in Athens,
a jointure that was equivalent to that left to Irini by

Niko, the opportunity to take her coveted degree, and every educational facility for Troy, if she would consent to live in Greece and let her son be brought up as the heir to the Alexiakis empire.

Laurel didn't interrupt as he made his offer, and her body relaxed a little. When he'd done she said, 'You didn't ask me to give him up, to let you and Irini take Troy over.'

'Because I knew you would never consent. And because the boy loves you too much; it would break his heart if he had to leave you.'

'Thank you for that.'

'And my offer? You will accept?'

He had deliberately made it so attractive that it would be hard not to. Laurel said, 'I'd be happy to accept the education for Troy when he's old enough—as a present from his grandfather.'

'And the rest?'

Slowly Laurel shook her head. 'I'm sorry, no. I don't want to stay in Greece. I want to go back to England. I appreciate your offer, Mr Alexiakis, but I have my own life to lead. I don't want to be just Troy's mother for the rest of my life, and dependent on your charity.'

'It would not be charity, it would be a—a wage, if you like, for looking after Troy.'

'I don't need a wage for looking after my own son! And let's face it, Mr Alexiakis: if Niko hadn't died and he and Irini had had children, you wouldn't even have looked at Troy. You would have wished him out of the way, the same as you did when he was conceived.'

Petros's swarthy face flushed and his thick eyebrows drew into a frown. 'Everyone makes mistakes, Laurel. But they can try to atone for them.'

She nodded gravely. 'And you have tried, very handsomely. But I'm sorry, I don't want to live in Greece. I realise, though, that you've become very attached to Troy and he to you, so I would be willing to bring him here for holidays every year. He could even come by himself when he's old enough. And, as you would be paying for his education, I would, of course, consult you at every stage. I'm willing to *share* my son with you, Mr Alexiakis, but I am not willing to change our lives completely for your sake.'

Petros opened his mouth to protest, but saw the steady determination in Laurel's eyes. Changing his tack, he said, 'You will go back to being a servant? You will let my grandson live in the basements of other people's houses? The boy who will one day rule the Alexiakis empire?'

Laurel bit her inner lip, knowing that he had found her weakness. 'If the idea offends you then I will try to get another job.'

'*Ochi!* No.' Petros slammed his fist down on the desk. 'I will not have this. You will take all or nothing. I will not have my grandson living in this way.'

'OK, nothing, then.' Laurel stood up. 'We managed before you came along and we can manage without you now.'

Petros shoved himself to his feet, gesturing angrily with his whole arms. 'Can you not see what shame it would bring to him when he is older? To know that there are people who knew him as the son of a servant, of a working woman?'

'And whose fault is that?' Laurel demanded, growing angry herself. 'If you'd let Niko and me get married Troy would have been brought up the way you wanted from the beginning.'

'So this is why you refuse me—because I kept you and Niko apart? It is revenge.'

'No!' Laurel's anger changed to irritation with herself. 'No, it isn't that at all. I'm sorry I said it. The past is over and done with.' Rallying, she added, 'But I don't think that it will do Troy any harm to see and experience how the working class live. Maybe it will make him more human, more sympathetic to other people.'

It would have been difficult for Petros not to see that remark as a criticism. Stiffly he said, 'I am offering everything you could want for you and your son; how can you refuse it for him, if not for yourself?'

'I can,' Laurel said stubbornly, trying to push out of her mind the fact that one of her reasons for doing so was because she never wanted to see Ross again.

Petros glared at her. 'So you care nothing for your son. You will let Troy grow up in poverty when he——'

'You called him Troy,' Laurel interrupted, her eyes wide with surprise.

'So? That is his name.'

'Yes, but I've never heard you use it before. You've always called him "the boy".'

'And you dislike this?' He gave her a puzzled look.

'Yes, because I've always been afraid that you see him as just another Niko. That you will try and take his identity away from him and bring him up in the same way.' Giving Petros a straight look, she said,

'And Niko wasn't happy. He was too afraid of you, too much under your thumb.'

'Of course Niko was happy. He had everything he wanted. What do you know of it?'

Laurel shook her head sadly. 'Not everything he wanted. He had my photo in his wallet when he died. And Irini didn't love him.'

Petros looked at her for long seconds and then slowly sat down. 'I made mistakes with Niko, I admit that. When a man has only one son he expects much from him.' He hesitated, obviously finding it difficult to go on. 'I see in Troy my chance to try again. To do it right. And—when Niko died, I thought my heart had died too. But your son—Troy, he has given me back my heart.' His voice grew husky. 'For my sake, for Niko's sake, please let me help Troy, and you.'

Laurel looked away, a lump in her throat, then went to her chair on the other side of the desk and sat down again. 'All right—but I won't live in Greece.'

Petros ran a hand across his sweating forehead, and now that she had capitulated seemed suddenly tired and middle-aged. 'I will have Stavros draw up an agreement as soon as he gets back. It shall be exactly as you want.'

'Thank you.' Unable to resist, she asked, 'Why do you call him Stavros and not Ross?'

Perhaps he noticed some tension in her voice, because Petros gave her a swift look. 'Stavros is his name.' He didn't explain further and might just as well have said nothing at all. She rose to go, but turned quickly when Petros, anxious that she shouldn't change her mind, said, 'I will telephone Stavros at once. He can pick up the boat at Piraeus or Naxos and will be here tomorrow.'

Laurel found Troy outside in the pool with Irini. He had soon learnt to swim and could already do several widths. Irini looked up at Laurel expectantly, knowing full well what her interview with Petros must have been about. 'It is all settled between you?'

Laurel nodded and sat down on a lounger. Before they could talk she had to watch Troy swim another width and listen to his account of all he'd been doing that morning. But then he allowed her to wrap a towel round him and settled into the crook of her arm for a nap.

'What happened?' Irini asked eagerly.

'We came to an agreement. I will let him have most of what he wants, but I refused to live in Greece. I want Troy to be brought up in England, but he is to come here for holidays.' But this wasn't what Irini was so eager to hear. Throwing her a smile, Laurel said, 'It's all right, your name wasn't even mentioned. You're free to—to marry, Irini.' Painfully she added, 'And I should tell you that Ross is coming back. He will be here tomorrow.'

'On the boat?' The other girl leaned forward eagerly. 'Is he coming on the *Irini*?'

'Why, yes.' Laurel gave her a surprised look. 'Petros said that it could pick him up either at Piraeus or Naxos; wherever he gets a flight to, I suppose.'

'But that's wonderful.' Irini's face lit. 'Then I will be able to tell Fotis.'

'Fotis? Who's he?'

Irini blushed. 'Fotis Andreas. The man I told you about.'

'You mean *Captain Andreas*?' Laurel stared at her open-mouthed. 'You're in love with *him*?'

The blush grew deeper as Irini smiled and nodded. 'But yes, I told you.'

'But I thought . . .' Laurel suddenly began to laugh. 'You didn't tell me his name. I thought you were in love with *Ross*.'

'Stavros?' Irini looked startled. 'Ah, no. Stavros is very nice, very handsome, but I could not marry him; I want to be free of the Alexiakis family.' Tilting her head, she gave Laurel a shrewd look. 'But I think you're quite pleased that I am not in love with Stavros.'

'You could say that,' Laurel agreed, unable to hide her sudden happiness. 'But didn't you try to get Ross alone that first night we were here?'

'I wanted to ask him what *your* plans were; if he knew whether you were going to leave Troy here and I would have to look after him.'

'Oh, I see. And did you go to say goodbye to— er—Fotis the night before they left?'

Irini blushed furiously and said quickly, 'How did you know?'

'I saw you go through the garden.'

Irini put a hand on her arm. 'Please, no one must know until my year of mourning is over. Petros would be very offended if he knew.'

'Of course I won't tell him.'

'And you won't tell Stavros? He might tell his—he might tell Petros.'

'Don't worry, I won't tell anyone, not even Ross; although I'm sure he wouldn't go sneaking to Mr Alexiakis even if he is his employer.'

Irini looked as if she was going to say something, but then she changed her mind and stood up excitedly. 'I must go and arrange for the hairdresser to come tomorrow morning. Do you wish her to do your hair?'

'Thanks, but I think I can manage.' Laurel wasn't keen on the rather sculptured style that seemed to be the only one the island hairdresser could do.

She sat back when Irini had gone, glad to be by herself. Oh, what a *fool* she'd been. And what a tease Ross must have thought her, blowing first hot and then cold. No wonder he'd been angry with her and had gone away. But he would be back tomorrow and somehow she would have to try and put everything right.

The rest of that day and the next seemed very long. Petros took Troy out fishing again and didn't invite the girls along; fishing was evidently an all-male sport. In some ways Laurel was pleased, because it meant she had lots of time to hope and dream, but in others she was sorry because looking after Troy would have given her something to do. Not having any idea when the *Irini* would arrive, and neither of them daring to ask Petros in case it betrayed their eager interest, Laurel and Irini spent most of the day sitting on the terrace where they could see the port in the distance. But no familiar boat came in before dark.

Laurel dressed very carefully for dinner that evening, putting on a beautiful cream silk dress that enhanced the golden tan she had acquired in the past two weeks. Irini, too, looked striking in a new dress, although she was restricted to the black and grey of mourning.

The meal, drawn out as a Greek meal normally was, had almost finished when there was a noise of voices outside in the hall and then Ross came into the room.

'Good evening.' His eyes went over them and rested on Laurel for a moment. 'I'm sorry to interrupt.'

'No, you don't interrupt.' Petros waved an ex-
pansive hand. 'Come and join us. Have you eaten?'

'Yes, thanks. They gave me a meal on the plane.'
Coming over to the table, he shook first Irini's hand,
then Laurel's, his glance meeting hers and widening
a little at what he read there. Then he shook hands
with Petros, who stood up to welcome him, gripping
his arm in surprising good-humour.

'At least have a coffee.'

They all went into the sitting-room and Thespina
brought in the coffee with an extra cup for Ross, an-
ticipating Petros's order. Ross took two filled cups
from her, giving one to Irini and bringing the other
over to Laurel. 'How are you?' he asked, his grey
eyes slightly wary, asking a different question.

'I'm fine, thank you. And you?'

He nodded. 'I'm well.' He glanced towards the
garden. 'It's a warm evening.'

'Yes.' Laurel's throat constricted, recognising his
message. Her voice even huskier than normal, she
said, 'Yes, it is.'

Impatiently, Petros broke in. 'Stavros, let's go to
my study. We have business to discuss.'

'Very well.' In contrast, Ross showed no im-
patience as he followed Petros out of the room.

As soon as they'd gone, Irini jumped to her feet,
her face animated. 'I am going to meet Fotis.'

Laurel finished her coffee and had another, making
it last, but Ross and Petros didn't come back. After
half an hour she went to check on Troy and then went
out into the garden. There was no need for a coat
tonight; as Ross had said, it was very warm. The faint
sound of *bouzouki* music floated up from the town
and Laurel could imagine Irini with her big bearded

sea-captain. She wished them happiness. She wished even more for her own.

It was almost another half an hour before Ross came. Laurel heard his footsteps first, hurrying along the path, and she stood up nervously. He halted at the end of the path, framed by a trellis supporting the bougainvillaea, his eyes probing the darkness. Laurel moved forward into a patch of moonlight, and he walked slowly towards her. He stopped again when he was a foot away, his eyes searching her face. 'Am I right in what I'm thinking?'

She smiled a little. 'If you're thinking that I missed you, then, yes, you are right.'

Laurel waited for him to take her in his arms but Ross held back, saying, 'You were angry with me when I left.'

'I know.' She hesitated. 'I thought you and Irini— I thought you were going to marry her.'

'What?' Ross gave an incredulous gasp. 'What on earth gave you that idea?'

'It was a misunderstanding.'

He didn't ask for an explanation. His eyes holding hers, Ross said thickly, 'And now that the misunderstanding is out of the way?'

'So, now I'm—very glad that you're back.'

Ross laughed richly. 'Well, that, at least, is a start.' And this time he pulled her into his arms and kissed her with all the pent-up longing of frustrated passion.

'Oh, Laurel, I've missed you. I've missed you.' He rained avid kisses on her eyes, her throat. 'There hasn't been a moment when I haven't thought about you, longed for you.'

'And I you. Oh, Ross, hold me close.'

His arms tightened as he kissed her again. 'I'm not going to let you go again, my darling.'

'You shouldn't have gone away. You should have stayed.' Laurel put her arms round his neck, her fingers in his hair as she pressed herself against him, her body filled with a burning ache of desire.

'I had to go. I had to let you know your own heart. You saw me only as Petros's messenger boy, a bringer of bad news. I *had* to take the risk of standing aside so that you could either miss me or forget me.' He smiled down at her, his features silvered by the moonlight. 'And it seems it was worth the risk.'

'Oh, *yes*. I was such a fool to think——'

Ross put a long finger over her lips. 'It's past.' His eyes, dark with yearning, gazed into hers. 'I love you, Laurel. My darling, darling girl.'

Her heart too full, her voice too choked with emotion to speak, Laurel put her hands on either side of his face and reached up to kiss him. It was a long kiss of joy and gratitude, but soon Ross's lips became compulsive, demanding, sending Laurel whirling again into a maelstrom of sensuous desire. His hands were hot on her bare skin, tantalising when he touched and caressed her, the hardness of his body creating an empty yearning deep inside her that longed for fulfilment. She gave a small moan that was a mighty shout for love.

'I want you.' Ross's voice was a gasping breath against her throat. 'I want to take off your clothes and look at you and love you.'

Drawing away a little, Laurel gave him a wild look, her lips parted and panting with urgent desire. 'I want that, too. Oh, Ross, I love you. I need you so much.'

Swinging her up in his arms, Ross carried her quickly across the garden to the changing-rooms beside the pool, then up the stairs to a guest suite only used when the house was full. The room, the bed when he laid her naked upon it, smelt of sun-filled flowers from the garden, of lemon trees and rich-scented jasmine. Laurel opened her arms to him and for the second time in her life gave herself uninhibitedly in whole-hearted love and trust.

CHAPTER EIGHT

DAWN was breaking when they made their way back to the house, their progress slow because Ross couldn't resist stopping to kiss Laurel yet again. 'My darling. My little love.' There was exultance in his voice, a new happiness in his eyes. At the fountain he stopped for the third time, but, instead of kissing her, put his hands up to cup her face. 'My sweet Laurel. Will you marry me, my love?'

Her breath caught and she looked at him with eyes filled with the radiant memories of the most wonderful night of her life. 'Of course I will.' Laurel clung to him, her eyes wet with tears of joy.

They kissed again but when they parted saw that they were bathed in a shaft of golden sunlight.

'We'd better get back,' Ross said ruefully. He led her to the house and they crept in, hoping that no one was awake. He came with her to her door and whispered, 'We'll talk in the morning. Sleep well, my love.' He put his hand low on her hip as he spoke, having every right to such a casually intimate touch now.

'Goodnight.' They kissed again, lingeringly, before Ross dragged himself away with a groan.

Laurel took off her clothes and smiled as she saw the faint marks on her body where Ross had held her as his body had surged with savage, primitive excitement. She decided not to sleep, to lie awake and remember every moment of that wonderful night, and then fell instantly asleep as soon as she got into bed.

She slept right through breakfast in the morning, but leapt out of bed as soon as she wakened and realised the time. 'Troy?' Laurel ran into his room, but he wasn't there. Quickly she showered and dressed and went to look for him. She found him at the outdoor pool with Irini.

'He has been very grown up,' the Greek girl told her. 'He saw you were asleep so he dressed himself and came for his breakfast. You must have been very tired,' Irini remarked, giving her an arch look.

Laurel blushed obligingly. 'Yes. Er—Ross and I had a lot to talk about. As I expect you and Fotis did?'

Irini gave a crow of laughter. 'I don't think we *talked* for as long as you. Petros has gone down to the village and won't be back until this evening.' She gestured towards the garden. 'And I think Ross has gone for a walk. Don't worry about Troy; I will look after him.'

Laurel gave her a warm smile. 'Thanks, Irini, you're a pal.'

Ross was leaning on the wall that edged the garden, looking out over the sea, but swung round when he heard her footsteps. 'Laurel!' He stepped forward and drew her into the shadow of an orange tree as he kissed her. 'Miss me?'

She shook her head teasingly. 'I fell fast asleep.'

'Did you dream about me, then?' he demanded.

She shook her head, but then laughed and put her arms round his neck. 'Every minute. Every single minute.'

That earned her another kiss until Ross said, 'And do you remember that you promised to marry me? You haven't changed your mind since you've slept so soundly on it?'

'No, of course not, but . . .' She drew away a little, her smile fading.

'What is it?'

'What about Troy? Has Petros told you? I've refused to give him up and leave him in Greece.'

'He didn't have to tell me that; I knew you wouldn't.'

'And that's OK? You'll take Troy along with me?'

Ross smiled and put his arm round her waist. 'I wouldn't have it any other way. I'm very fond of Troy, you know that.'

Laurel gave a small sigh of perfect contentment. 'There are some men who wouldn't want to take on an illegitimate child.'

'I'm the last one to demur at that.' He hesitated, then said rather ruefully, 'As it happens, I'm illegitimate myself.'

'You are?' Laurel looked at him in total surprise. She waited for him to go on, but when he didn't she said, 'Is that why you haven't told me much about your family? You're not—ashamed, are you?' But she couldn't somehow think of Ross's ever being ashamed of what couldn't be changed.

And he justified her opinion as he said, 'Good heavens, no. But there's nothing to be proud of either. I'm the product of a long-term liaison between my mother and a man who is now dead. The affair started when the man's wife was still alive but when she died he acknowledged me and I was brought up more or less as his son, but as he refused to marry my mother I was never completely part of his family. Even though he wouldn't marry her my mother stayed with him, mostly for my sake, I think, until he died. Then she took off.'

'And you went with her?'

Ross shook his head. 'I was nearly twenty; I'd already left.'

Quick to sympathise, Laurel said, 'It must have been a very unhappy boyhood for you.'

'At times.' A nostalgic look came into Ross's eyes. 'At others it was wonderful and I wouldn't have changed it for any other kind of life.' He smiled at her. 'So you see, you have no need to worry about Troy.'

'What about the offer Petros made me? I agreed to let him help us and for Troy to visit him. Did he tell you that last night?'

'Yes, he did. But you won't need his help now; I'll take care of you both.'

'I don't think he'll like it. It would mean that he'll have less—control over Troy.'

'And is that a bad thing?'

'No, I suppose not. But what about his schooling? I told Petros that I'd accept his offer to pay for that.'

Ross pulled her to him and kissed her forehead. 'Darling, will you let me legally adopt Troy when we're married? That way you'll have complete control of his upbringing. You won't have to worry about Petros.'

'But I promised,' Laurel said with a frown.

'That was yesterday; things are different now.'

And how different; Laurel realised that her whole life, her whole future had changed overnight. And oh, how wonderfully! She smiled mistily at Ross and lifted her hand to stroke his face gently. 'But perhaps I'll still let Troy come here for holidays. I can't refuse Petros even that. Especially if he makes Troy his heir.'

'We'll do just as you want.' Ross's voice had thickened at her touch. Turning his head, he pressed his mouth into her palm, kissing it with warm, ardent kisses. 'You beautiful minx. I'm crazy in love with you.'

He pulled her to him, his hands low on her hips so that she could feel the hardening of his body. Laurel gave a breathless laugh. 'Already?'

'Always. Don't you know I can't get enough of you?' He took her hand, his eyes dark with desire. 'Come on, let's go to the guest house.'

She didn't resist, couldn't. And this time it was Laurel who slowly undressed Ross, gently exploring him with her lips and her hands as she did so, until his body was bathed in a soft sweat of sensuous anticipation. He lay on the bed and watched as Laurel took off her clothes and came to join him. Then, unable to wait any longer, he fiercely pulled her down on top of him.

Later, much later, they lay close in each other's arms, their sexual desires satiated for the moment. Laurel gave a purr of sheer contentment, but after a while sighed and said, 'But what about Petros? Will you tell him or shall I?'

To her relief Ross said at once, 'I'll tell him. But not yet. Let's keep it our secret for a while. OK?'

'Oh, yes.' It more than suited Laurel. She, too, didn't want their blissful happiness spoiled by Petros's inevitable anger.

Everything blew up a couple of days later. Petros had been preoccupied with business in the village, where a lot of the younger men wanted to enlarge the harbour so that they could have bigger fishing boats, while others were against the change. As the owner of the island, Petros had to mediate, and so he was away from the house a lot, giving Ross and Laurel long, precious hours together. Irini, too, took advantage of his absence and used Troy as her excuse to go down to the boat and go sailing each day with Fotis Andreas. But, the harbour problems settled, Petros turned his attention again to the contract that Ross was supposed to be drawing up about Troy's future.

His roar of anger when he was told that things had changed was so loud that Laurel and Irini, sitting outside by the pool, heard it. They looked at each other apprehensively. Laurel stood up. 'Ross must have told him.'

'Told him what?'

'About Ross and me. That we're engaged to be married.' Laurel was unable to keep the happy blush from her cheeks.

'It has gone that far?'

'Why, yes. You must have guessed. What else did you expect?' Laurel stopped, realising that because of her past affair with Niko Irini might well have thought that she and Ross were just indulging in a holiday romance. 'I'd better go in there. I can't let Ross face him alone.'

Irini caught her wrist. 'No, don't.' She, too, came to her feet. 'Petros is bound to be terribly angry. He could not have foreseen this. If he had suspected he would have sent you and Troy away at once.'

'Or more likely Ross,' Laurel said nervously, her eyes on the window of the study.

'But he can't order Stavros away; not his own brother.'

For a moment Laurel didn't take it in, her mind on the shouts of rage coming from the house. Then she turned slowly to stare at Irini. 'Do you mean Ross? Are you saying that—that Ross is Petros's *brother*?'

'Why, yes,' Irini's eyes searched her face. 'Hasn't he told you?'

'No,' Laurel said hollowly. 'He forgot to mention that.' Shaking off Irini's hand, she said, 'Take care of Troy for me,' and ran towards the house.

'Laurel! Come back. You should not interfere.'

But Laurel took no notice of Irini's warning and ran to the study. Jerking open the door, she saw the two men facing each other across the width of Petros's desk. Petros was furious, shouting and raging, but Ross was completely calm, a look of cold triumph on his lean, handsome face. When he saw her Ross reached out a hand and pulled her to his side. 'She's mine,' he said to Petros in Greek. 'Her and the boy. Your little game has backfired on you.'

Petros swore at him, his language earthy. 'You've used the girl's need for a man to make her break her promises to me. You think by marrying her and adopting the boy you'll make sure that you get your hands on everything I've got, but I'll see you rot in hell first. You bastard!'

'That's fact, not insult,' Ross returned coldly. Mockingly he said, 'You really should weigh up all the possibilities before you start trying to impose your will on people, Petros. Sometimes they have a will of their own.'

'I'll disown the boy!'

'Go ahead. Then I'll inherit everything,' Ross goaded.

'Damn you to hell!' Petros became aware of Laurel. 'That little tramp. I'll give her money to stay away from you, enough to buy her a dozen lovers.'

'It wouldn't work,' Ross said on a sneer. 'She's in love with me.' Reverting to English he said to Laurel, 'You are in love with me, aren't you, darling?'

Laurel suddenly wrenched her arm free and hit out at him. 'Damn you! Damn you both! How *dare* you treat Troy and me as pawns in some sort of game? You made a big mistake, both of you, letting me hear what you said. Because I speak Greek and I understood every word.' She glared at them, ignoring the consternation in their eyes. 'You were just using us for your own ends.' She rounded on Petros. 'You didn't really care about Troy at all; all you were interested in was stopping Ross from inheriting your money. And as for *you*!' Laurel swung round to face Ross. 'You're utterly despicable. I thought—I *really* thought you loved me, when all the time...' She couldn't go on, her voice was too choked with anger to speak.

'Laurel, wait,' Ross said urgently. 'Don't get the wrong idea. I only wanted to——'

'It's perfectly obvious what you wanted,' Laurel said bitterly. 'Petros's fortune. Either for yourself or through Troy. Well, you can fight it out between you, because I'm not going to stay here and be used by either of you any longer. You're both—odious!' And she ran out of the room, slamming the door behind her.

She heard Ross shout her name, and then Petros's voice, but Laurel took no notice. Running into the garden, she grabbed up Troy.

'Laurel, what happened?' Irini followed her inside.

'We're leaving.' Reaching their suite, she lugged out her suitcase and began to throw some of the clothes they'd brought with them into it.

'Mummy?' Troy raised a frightened face to her.

Trying to hide her rage for his sake, Laurel said, 'It's all right, darling. We're going home to England, that's all.'

'Why?'

'Yes, why?' Irini demanded.

'I'll tell you later. Here, put your other shoes on, Troy.'

There was a sharp rap at the door and Ross strode in. 'Laurel, I have to speak to you.'

'Go away.'

His voice like steel, Ross said shortly, 'Irini, take Troy and wait outside.'

'Stay where you are,' Laurel countered, fastening Troy's shoes. 'Put your jacket on, poppet.'

With an angry exclamation Ross stepped forward. 'You've got to listen to me.'

'Listen to you! You must be joking.' Putting on her own coat, she picked up the case and her handbag. 'Come on, Troy.'

'Wait.' Ross caught hold of Laurel's arm.

She gave him an icy, venomous stare. 'Take your filthy hand off me.'

'Laurel, you've got it all wrong.'

'Huh!' The sound was heavy with insult and contempt.

Biting back his anger, Ross pulled her round to face him. 'I'm not going to let you go until you've listened to what I have to say.'

'I don't want to hear. It would be nothing but lies anyway.'

'Well, you're damn well going to. The reason I——' He broke off abruptly as Laurel opened her mouth and screamed.

'Mummy!' Troy gave a cry of terror and clung to her leg.

Petros came running in. 'What are you doing to them?' He grabbed hold of Ross and pulled him away from her.

It looked as if a full-scale fight was about to develop, but Irini ran forward and started shouting at them to stop. Taking advantage of the confusion, Laurel grabbed Troy's hand and ran with him out of the house and down the road towards the village.

He was crying in bewilderment, as he had every right to. 'I'm sorry, darling,' Laurel tried to soothe him. 'Don't worry. We're going home. Let's see how quickly we can get down to the village, shall we?'

But they hadn't gone more than half a mile when footsteps came running behind them and Ross caught them up. He stopped in front of her, out of breath. His hair was dishevelled and there was a red mark on his jaw. 'Laurel, please.'

But she ignored him and tried to walk round him, pulling Troy along. He whimpered uncertainly.

Ross quickly got in front of them again and held out his arms, barring the way. 'Do you have to upset Troy like this?' he said forcefully.

Laurel glared at him. 'Trust a rat like you to make that remark. Get out of the way.'

'All right, if that's what you want,' he said curtly, his own anger rising. 'But not until you've listened to me.'

She was about to tell him to go to hell, but saw the fierce determination in his eyes and knew that this time she had no choice. 'So say what you've got to say,' she said furiously, in no mood to listen, determined to go on hating him.

Ross stood for a minute, getting his breath back, his eyes on her face. Grimly he said, 'I haven't lied to you, Laurel. I love you and I want to marry you.'

'Yes, so that you can get hold of Petros's money.'

'I don't give a damn about his money!' Ross said violently. 'I spent the first eighteen years of my life taking Alexiakis hand-outs because I had no choice. But I paid my own way through university and I've been paying my own way ever since. I neither want nor need Petros's money, because living on someone else's charity is no fun, believe me.'

'No? Then why did he say you were after it? Why did you say that if he disinherited Troy you would get everything? I understood, remember? And I know that you're lying through your teeth.'

'Because the way his father's—our father's—will is written, I do stand to inherit if Petros has no heir. Look, I know it's difficult to understand. The enmity between us goes back a long way. Petros knew that my mother was his father's mistress and was naturally angry about it on his own mother's behalf. He was even angrier when his father insisted that I be brought up as part of the family when his mother died.' Ross paused, took a deep breath. 'He was a lot older than me. He sometimes made life unbearable and he was often cruel. But we eventually came to respect each other and Petros used my company for his British business. We weren't friends by any means, but he knew he could trust me. I was family, you see.'

Laurel was listening and was angry at herself for doing so. She tried to go past him.

'I haven't finished yet. You can listen for another five minutes. You owe me that.'

'I don't owe you anything.'

Ross's grey eyes met hers and held them. 'Yes, you do.'

Laurel remembered the hours she had spent in his arms, the times he had lifted her to moaning heights of ecstasy, and quickly looked away.

'Petros and I would probably have gone on for the rest of our lives, meeting occasionally for business reasons, keeping each other at a distance. But then Niko died and everything changed. Suddenly I was his heir, and that was anathema to Petros. But he remembered Troy.'

Laurel began to argue despite herself. 'And sent you to find us? To persuade me to go to Greece? Send his heir to find someone to replace him? He would never have done that if what you say is true.'

'But he did, because he knew he could trust me. And also because it's the kind of sadistic touch he enjoys. As for me, I was only too anxious to find you and let him make Troy his heir; I didn't want Petros for an enemy; I just wanted to get back on our old footing.' He sighed and put a hand up to push his hair off his forehead. The mark on his jaw was turning a deeper red. 'I intended to find you, bring you here, and then leave you to sort it out between you.'

'So why didn't you?'

'Because I realised you were no match for Petros. Because I found that the liking I had for you when we first met when you were in love with Niko soon became a great deal more. I fell in love with you and I wanted to protect you and Troy. I didn't want to give Petros the chance of taking Troy over. He would have done, you know. He would have made you entirely dependent on him, the way his father made my mother dependent on *him*. The holidays here would have lengthened until you were spending most of your time in Greece. And if you had ever let Troy come here alone you would have had a great deal of difficulty getting him back.' Troy had gone to pick some flowers at the side of the road, but Ross dropped his voice so that the child couldn't hear.

'You must be mad if you expect me to believe that.'

'You have every right to be angry, Laurel. But all I wanted to do was to protect you and Troy and at the same time goad Petros into making Troy his heir, to spite me if for no other reason. But I think that Petros is genuinely fond of Troy because he's so like Niko.'

'Why hasn't he come after us, then?'

Amusement came briefly into Ross's eyes. 'He's nursing a swollen jaw.'

Laurel stiffened, refusing to be drawn. 'Have you finished?'

'Yes, I think so.' Ross looked at her intently.

'Then will you please get out of the way?'

His jaw tensed. 'Doesn't what I've said mean anything to you?'

'No, it doesn't.'

'And the love that we've shared; doesn't that count for anything either?'

'No, because it wasn't true. You were using me.'

His head came up, his jaw proud, and at that moment Ross looked very Greek. He stepped aside. 'Go, then. I'm not going to beg and plead. I've told you the truth. If you don't love me enough to believe me then there's no future for us. And if the last few days have meant so little to you then maybe it's best that you go.'

Laurel stared at him, hurt and confused, not knowing what to believe. She couldn't sort things out in her mind; everything had happened too quickly. Turning, she called out, 'Troy!' and held her hand out to her son.

He came obediently to her side. 'Is Ross coming? Can I have a piggyback?' he said hopefully.

'No, he isn't coming.' Keeping her head averted, Laurel continued her trudge to the village.

She half expected—half hoped?—that Ross would come after her again, but in only a few minutes she heard his footsteps as he turned to go back towards the house.

It was a long way to the village. They had never walked it before and it took them a long time because Troy was so slow. After a mile or so he grew tired and Laurel had to carry him as well as the case. The sun was going down as they reached the first of the houses. Laurel set Troy down, her arms aching, and took the stepped path that led directly down the steep hillside to the harbour. 'Here, we can have a rest now.' They sat on a bench overlooking the sea, a place where the fishermen mended their nets in the mornings. The place smelt strongly of fish and some of the scales trapped in the gutter shone like pearls in the evening sun.

'I'm hungry,' Troy informed her.

'All right, we'll find somewhere to eat.'

They walked along the sea front to a taverna that they'd visited before with Ross and the others. Laurel ordered some food for Troy but just a coffee for herself. Looking across the harbour, she saw the daily

ferry-boat from Naxos coming in. A lot of the
islanders worked in Naxos and came home every day.
It would stay for another hour or so, she knew. All
she had to do was to walk across and board it and
she would be able to shut this part of her life out
forever. Just forget it as if it had never been. But did
she really want that? Sitting at the rickety table, the
lights of the town gradually coming on, Laurel began
to go over all that had happened in the last few hours.
She tried to do so rationally, to weigh up all Ross's
arguments, but always it came back to feelings. She
remembered the glorious love they had shared. Could
that possibly have been so wonderful if it had been a
pretence? What if Ross had been telling the truth?
Could she possibly throw up that possibility because
her pride was hurt? And most of all—could she bear
to live without him?

Troy's head was sagging and his food had grown
cold. Leaning forward impulsively, knowing that the
child's instinct about people was invariably right, and
that his future was as much at stake as hers, she said,
'Troy, do you want to go back to England?'

He opened his eyes, trying to concentrate. 'Is Ross
coming?'

'No.' She shook her head.

'Then I don't want to go,' he said decidedly. 'I want
Ross.'

Laurel's face broke into a relieved, happy smile.
'And so do I.'

It would be a long walk back to the villa and Troy
was very tired. Going into the taverna, Laurel asked
to use the phone. Thespina answered, but when Laurel
asked for Ross the housekeeper said, 'I'm sorry, Miss

Marland, but Mr Stavros isn't here. He took the car and went out over an hour ago.'

'Oh, thank you.' Laurel slowly replaced the receiver. She could have asked for someone else to pick her up. There were other cars at the villa and Irini could drive, but she somehow felt that it would be wrong. It was Ross she wanted, Ross to whom she would go. 'Can I leave my case here, please?' she asked the proprietor, startling him with her fluency in Greek.

'But certainly, *kyria*. It will be safe here.'

She thanked him and went back to Troy. He was asleep, his head resting on his hands on the table. 'Come on, my darling, just one more walk and then we'll be safe forever.' Lifting him up in her arms, Laurel turned away from the waterfront where the ferry-boat was moored, and walked back through the town. Away from the lights it quickly grew dark. The road and the stepped path met at the corner of the church. A car was parked there, without any lights. As Laurel approached the door opened and Ross got out. He came towards her. Laurel stopped, her eyes anxiously searching his face. What she saw there filled her heart with joy and thankfulness.

'Need any help?'

She gave a tremulous smile. 'Yes, please.'

He took Troy from her and held him easily in his arms. 'I've been waiting. Watching to see if you decided to take the ferry. You took your time.'

Laurel put her arm through that of her golden Greek. Softly she said, 'Not when you compare it with the rest of my life.'

WIN A LUXURY CRUISE

TO THE MEDITERRANEAN
AND BLACK SEA

st month we told you all about the fabulous cruise you could win just by
tering our competition and sending in two tokens from November and
cember Romances.

r the lucky winner the popular cruise ship the Kareliya will be a floating hotel
iting eight exciting ports of call, including Lisbon, Athens and Istanbul.

r your chance to win this fabulous cruise for two people just answer these
ee questions and the tie-breaker which follows:

Which country is renowned for its delicious port? ....

Which volcano is situated on the island of Sicily? ....

Which Turkish city sits at the mouth of the Bosphorus? ....

e-Breaker. Tell us in no more than 15 words which romantic partner you
uld like to take on a cruise with you and why ....

....

....

me: ....

dress:..

....Postcode:...........................

e you a Reader Service subscriber?   Yes ☐   No ☐

 may be mailed with offers from other reputable companies as a result of this entry. If you do not wish to
eive such information please tick this box ☐.

nd your entry, together with two tokens, a red one from November and a blue
e from December Romances by 31st January 1992 to:

Holiday Competition   Mills & Boon Reader Service
P.O. Box 236   Thornton Road   Croydon   Surrey   CR9 3RU

From the author of Mirrors comes an enchanting romance

Caught in the steamy heat of America's New South, Rebecca Trenton finds herself torn between two brothers – she yearns for one, but a dark secret binds her to the other.

Off the coast of South Carolina lay Pirate's Bank – a small island as intriguing as the legendary family that lived there. As the mystery surrounding the island deepened, so Rebecca was drawn further into the family's dark secret – and only one man's love could save her from the treachery which now threatened her life.

W●RLDWIDE

Accept 4 Free Romances and 2 Free gifts

•FROM READER SERVICE•

An irresistible invitation from Mills & Boon Reader Service. Please accept our offer of 4 free Romances, a CUDDLY TEDDY and a special MYSTERY GIFT... Then, if you choose, go on to enjoy 6 captivating Romances every month for just £1.60 each, postage and packing free. Plus our FREE newsletter with author news, competitions and much more.

Send the coupon below to: Reader Service, FREEPOST, PO Box 236, Croydon, Surrey CR9 9EL.

--------------- NO STAMP REQUIRED ---------------

Yes! Please rush me my 4 Free Romances and 2 Free Gifts! Please also reserve me a Reader Service Subscription. If I decide to subscribe, I can look forward to receiving 6 new Romances every month for just £9.60, postage and packing is free. If I choose not to subscribe I shall write to you within 10 days - I can keep the books and gifts whatever I decide. I can cancel or suspend my subscription at any time. I am over 18 years of age.

Name Mrs/Miss/Ms/Mr ————————————————— EP17R

Address ————————————————————————————

Postcode ———————— Signature————————————

Next month's Romances

Each month, you can choose from a world of variety in romance with Mills & Boon. These are the new titles to look out for next month.

DESPERATE MEASURES Sara Craven

STRANGER FROM THE PAST Penny Jordan

FATED ATTRACTION Carole Mortimer

A KIND OF MAGIC Betty Neels

A CANDLE FOR THE DEVIL Susanne McCarthy

TORRID CONFLICT Angela Wells

LAST SUMMER'S GIRL Elizabeth Barnes

DESERT DESTINY Sarah Holland

THE CORSICAN GAMBIT Sandra Marton

GAMES FOR SOPHISTICATES Diana Hamilton

SUBSTITUTE HUSBAND Margaret Callaghan

MIRROR IMAGE Melinda Cross

LOVE BY DESIGN Rosalie Ash

IN PURSUIT OF LOVE Jayne Bauling

NO LAST SONG Ann Charlton

STARSIGN

ENIGMA MAN Nicola West

Available from Boots, Martins, John Menzies, W.H. Smith, most supermarkets and other paperback stockists.

Also available from Mills and Boon Reader Service, P.O. Box 236, Thornton Road, Croydon, Surrey CR9 3RU.